corg

DANTE'S
PEAK

D0858885

DANTE'S PEAK

A NOVEL BY
DEWEY GRAM

BASED ON THE
MOTION PICTURE WRITTEN BY
LESLIE BOHEM

BOULEVARD BOOKS, NEW YORK

DANTE'S PEAK

A novel by Dewey Gram
Based on the motion picture written by Leslie Bohem

A Boulevard Book / published by arrangement with
MCA Publishing Rights, a Division of MCA, Inc.

PRINTING HISTORY
Boulevard edition / March 1997

The Putnam Berkley World Wide Web site address is
http://www.berkley.com/berkley

ISBN: 1-57297-270-X

BOULEVARD
Boulevard Books are published by The Berkley Publishing Group,
200 Madison Avenue, New York, New York 10016.
BOULEVARD and its logo are trademarks
belonging to Berkley Publishing Corporation.

PRINTED IN THE UNITED STATES OF AMERICA

10 9 8 7 6 5 4 3 2 1

1

Electrical charges built up in the mushrooming black clouds, and bolts of lightning cracked into the shrouded ground. A dark, sooty rain fell heavily on the tiny town, a rain not of water but of cindery volcanic debris and ash known as tephra.

A constant deep bass rumble, as of gigantic rocket engines struggling to break free, shook the earth. Sporadic shock waves from mammoth explosions blasted across the forest, bending and cracking the trees.

Overhead, just a glimmer of what would normally have been the noonday sun appeared for brief moments, then winked out into the darkness of raining ash. Day had disappeared.

Galeras was a village in southwestern Colombia. It huddled in the equatorial forests of the Andes Cordillera, the high, craggy spine of South America that had its beginnings here on the northwestern shoulder of the continent and ran the length of the Pacific Coast to Tierra del Fuego. The entire Cordillera was a child of tectonics—the folding, buckling, volcano-producing process that resulted when the edges of two of the earth's twenty or so gigantic crustal plates collided.

The ancient process, still going on underground at that moment, accounted for the mayhem going on above.

All along the western coast of the continent, the Nazca tectonic plate and the South American plate were crashing together, and the former was diving under the latter. At a certain depth the subducted Nazca plate was melting, sending up pipes of molten rock, the stuff of volcanoes.

In Galeras, one such subduction volcano was erupting, adding torment to the already tortured, twisted Andean terrain.

It was true that this was a landscape inhospitable in the extreme, and that it yielded little in the way of livelihood for the hardy Colombian Indians whose roots went thirty generations deep in the upthrust granite. But it was also true that the very harshness of the landscape amounted to a kind of blessing: Only a few hundred people lived in the immediate lee of the monster that was raining death.

Chaos gripped the town of Galeras, and terror animated the few hundred inhabitants as they scrambled to evacuate by foot, by truck, by bicycle—any way they could.

One outsider—one who should have known better than to be here at this dark hour—struggled to keep his battered Dodge pickup on the rutted road and get on with his own departure.

Harry Dalton, geologist-volcanologist, rushed frantically to cross the besieged town and get to his makeshift "volcano observatory" headquarters on the far side. Harry Dalton, sweating heavily as he navigated his truck, knew that he was pushing his luck—again.

Harry had been Trouble from the age of short pants, if you asked his mother. "Stubborn" was too mild a word. And it wouldn't have done to even talk to his father about Harry; their standard way of conversing since Harry was a teenager had been pitched battle.

Had Harry, now in his mid-thirties, chosen the life expected of him—the suit, the tie, and the laptop on the commuter train—he might have been thought handsome, almost too handsome. He had long since taken care of that. If he shaved once every four days when he was in the field it was unusual. If he exposed his weather-beaten face to the high-altitude sun, wind, and dust less than three-quarters of every year, it was a bad year.

No, people didn't think of Harry as handsome, but more as a determined, demanding, driven SOB with a smile that could light the room if the thought occurred to him.

And the thought occurred to him only rarely. Most of the time he was too busy grimacing in intense concentration in pursuit of the passion of his life, volcanoes. Occasionally, when Harry's labors in a dormant caldera yielded an intriguing finding, or when the prospect of facing a live volcano reared up, his face would light up with a look of hard-bitten joy, like that of a boy who had discovered Red Beard's treasure all on his own.

Harry slewed the pickup around a mudslide and gunned toward the far end of the small village. Now as he shot a look through his windshield up into the mountains to the west, his expression of hard-bitten joy was tinged with a certain dread.

He pulled up in front of a small adobe brick building, left the engine running, and rushed inside.

In the one-room dirt-floored dwelling, with nothing resembling plumbing and only cloth for windowpanes, were signs of the late twentieth century: two computers and, hooked up to them, a pair of near state-of-the-art portable field seismographs.

This was the United States Geological Survey's Colombia Station—Temporary Observatory.

Monitoring the seismographs was Marianne, a beautiful, slim, athletic young woman and Harry's wife-to-be. She was excitedly annotating the readouts with personal observations as tremors rocked the building and red dust cascaded from the cracked ceiling. She was chattering with her two Colombian assistants in Indian dialect, directing them in covering the windows and computers with plastic sheets to keep out the dust and ash, when Harry burst in.

"Honey, let's get the hell out of here," Harry said. "Now!"

The two Indian boys didn't have to be told twice, and they flew past Harry out the door. But when Marianne turned to him from the seismographs, there was that gleam in her eyes.

"Let's stick around, Harry," she said. "Let's see the show."

Harry understood. Of course he did. Hell, before he'd met Marianne, it would have been him saying those exact words. "The show"—it was a main reason why he, a marriage-averse, better-off-as-a-bachelor, inveterate lone ranger if ever there was one, had fallen so hard for Marianne when they met at a site in Alaska two years before.

2

Marianne Satterfield was as avid a volcano junkie as Harry Dalton. She was as much turned on by proximity to an active volcano's secrets and power as he was. She was a woman who not only was not afraid of a volcano's rumble, but who came alive at the sensation. "It takes over your body," she said to Harry at that first encounter.

Harry's eyes went wide. Here was a woman who was attractive, yes. By reputation, a first-rate field scientist, yes. But suddenly she was so much more: a gorgeous human seismograph. And she *understood*.

Harry was hooked. He had found his soul mate. He proposed before they had even left the site. Marianne was levelheaded enough to postpone her answer until they were back on solid ground and she could make a sensible judgment: Was it Harry or Pele the Volcano Goddess who was moving her to fall in love?

It was Harry.

They had planned to get married in her hometown of Baltimore, but had had to postpone the rites several times because of juicy assignments. Three weeks ago they were finally on their way to Baltimore for the small family wedding when this unlikely volcano in Colombia had started to rumble.

They immediately postponed the ceremony again and headed to USGS headquarters in Vancouver, Washington. They walked into their boss's office ready to go—only to be told the USGS was going to pass on this one as small potatoes in probable magnitude and as posing very little danger to population, so remote was the site.

Marianne was not to be denied.

They put their heads together and connived. While Harry kept up a steady barrage of argument that the USGS should send them for purely scientific reasons, Marianne quietly went to work.

She contacted officials she knew at British Petroleum Ltd., Oxy Colombia, Shell, and Occidental Petroleum of Bakersfield, California, all of whom had major pipelines running through the Cordillera in Colombia. Oil production in the Colombia fields was up, she knew, and she'd heard they were considering building new pipelines. She convinced the officials they needed to know the volcano risks of the area. The oil companies gladly agreed to jointly pay 80 percent of the costs of the research, no strings attached.

Colombia, here we come. Wedding later.

They had just begun planting seismometers and wiring this simmering volcano when it suddenly went hot much faster than they'd ever expected.

Now, nothing but concern for Marianne could have made Harry say and do what he never had before at the site of a venting volcano: "We've waited too long already," he barked commandingly. "We're going now. Come on." He grabbed her hand. If Harry was being this adamant, Marianne thought, there must be urgent cause for concern. She knew she had no choice but to rush out with him.

They raced toward the truck, where the assistants were waiting. Just as they neared the vehicle a volcanic bomb exploded close to them—a chunk of semisolidified lava blown from the spewing crater two miles away. The bomb threw up a pile of earth like a mortar explosion right behind them, slamming them forward into the truck. The Indian assistants took off running toward the hills. Harry sprinted, dragged them back, and pushed them into the rear of the pickup.

The mountain was roaring as Harry slammed the truck into gear and drove through the central square of the town. He had to pick his way carefully through the fleeing Indians. Absolute pandemonium reigned on the streets—old people wandering lost, women with babes in arms running in a down-mountain direction as fast as they could, pulling and dragging toddlers after them.

Harry wound his way onto the steep, muddy mountain road. Behind them, another huge explosion shook the earth as a section on a shoulder of the cone blew off and a second crater opened.

The shock wave rolled down the mountain, flattening trees. Harry had to fight to keep the truck on the road. The two assistants in the back held on tight as they were slammed from side to side. Far up the mountain behind them they watched in horror as a lahar—a torrent of hot volcanic mud—rushed down toward their village.

As the truck reached a relatively straight stretch and sped up, a volcanic bomb crashed into the ground in front of it. Harry rode the truck up over the lava rock, nearly tipping the vehicle over. Then another bomb slammed directly onto the front fender, buckling it, causing smoke to billow as metal and tire came into contact.

Harry hunched over the wheel and drove for his life—for *all* their lives. Marianne, her face flushed with adrenaline, turned around to look back through the rear window. The sky behind was black with dense ashfall. The truck raced crazily, slamming and bouncing around curves. The assistants hung on desperately, choking on the gas-laden air.

Then a small volcanic bomb, no bigger than a grapefruit, smashed through the roof of the cab.

Harry turned to see Marianne slump forward in the seat. Blood seeped from the back of her head. Harry clutched her lifeless body to him, driving as fast as he could, unwilling to believe. "Oh Marianne, oh my God. Hang on, girl. Oh my God . . ."

His cries of agony melded with the litany of volcanic bombs landing all around them and the screaming engine of the truck as Harry pushed it to its limits, trying to reach help for his beloved Marianne.

3

The Cascades Vancouver Observatory of the United States Geological Survey was a squat, deceptively unimposing two-story building. Cinder-block construction, marching rows of identical windows. It looked more like a low-income apartment complex than the brain center of the largest organization in the world devoted to the study of volcanoes and the prediction of their eruption.

Harry Dalton walked down an echoing corridor. He had aged since Galeras and the death of his fiancée. Something detached, a little distant, now shone in his eyes. The world was no longer the win-win proposition it had been.

Nine people had died at Galeras: three locals, five volcanologists from other teams, and Marianne. But Harry and Marianne's mission had yielded results.

Galeras got put on a list of fifteen volcanoes worldwide being monitored by the scientific community as "International Decade Volcanos." Meaning it was now viewed as a volcano big and dangerous enough to bear constant watching, because it represented significant hazard to the population of the city of Pasto, population three hundred thousand, eight kilometers away. Now the space shuttle, starting with one of the Endeavor missions, regularly photographed it using space-borne imaging radar and heat-sensitive infrared, looking for changes, red flags.

It was a bitter accomplishment for Harry. Any gratification he might have felt as a scientist was buried in anguish with his love.

He headed down the hall and rounded the corner and was about to hit the staircase when—climbing slowly, awkwardly up the staircase toward him—Spider Legs reared its blunt head.

The creature was a four-foot-tall walking tethered robot with a blocky temperature-resistant ceramic-metal body and eight legs—four each sprouting from two track-mounted frames. The legs had suction cups at the telescoping rubberoid "ankles." The "feet" extended four inches past the cups. The robot "walked" by having one frame first lift its legs off the ground, slide forward, plant its legs on the ground, and redistribute the center of gravity so that the other frame could lift its legs and slide forward.

Terry Furlong, a big guy with a rusty brown beard

11

and a penchant for loud shirts, was the mechanical engineer/volcanologist who had built Spider Legs. He stood at the foot of the stairs maneuvering the robot with a remote control. Two technicians, Nancy Field, a pretty woman in her mid-twenties, and Stan Tzima, a couple of years older, cheered the mechanical arachnid on.

"Come on, Spider Legs," Terry shouted. "Do it for Daddy."

Harry, stepping aside for Spider Legs, noticed the small oblong metal box rigged on struts to the robot's back. "What's with the hump?" he said.

"That hump there," Stan said, "is what keeps us raking in those NASA grants. If we want their money we have to test out some of their stuff like ELF here."

"Elf?" Harry said.

"E.L.F." Terry said. "Extralow-frequency transmitter. ELF's the gizmo that sent sound waves through the planet and came up with the new stuff about the iron core spinning faster than the rest of the earth. She'll tell 'em what Mars is actually made out of. Like anybody gives a flying—Damnit!" He gave the joystick to Stan and heaved his burly body toward the stairs. "There you go again," he barked at the robot. "How do you expect to walk into a volcano if you can't even walk on the stairs?"

Spider Legs had stopped walking. He just stood there flailing. Terry mounted the steps and gave the robot a good swift kick in the rear. "Sorry, pal," he said. Spider Legs responded to the tough love. He got going again, slowly executing his ungainly steps up the stairs.

"Quasimodo here was taking the stairs two at a time before they made Terry put the ELF on its back," Nancy said.

Harry was interested. He moved in for a closer look. "Hmm—changes the machine's center of gravity," he said, "and clearly too much weight to carry at earth gravity. Let's see what happens if we take it off? Maybe it just has to be repositioned." Harry had that intense look of a problem junkie faced with a ripe challenge. He was literally rolling up his sleeves when Terry cut him off good-naturedly.

"The only thing taking off is you," he said. "You've got a plane to catch, remember?"

"You lucky dog," Nancy said. "Heading off for the Keys."

Harry keenly felt the irony of the remark, insofar as it only crystallized the realization that he did not want to be going on vacation. That he was less than thrilled to be headed for marlin fishing in the Keys when he knew, for a fact, that among the fifteen hundred active volcanoes in the world, eight to twelve eruptions were occurring *at that moment*. And that if he were at any one of them he would be learning something valuable and startling.

He started tinkering with Spider Legs. "There's plenty of time," he said distractedly.

Stan had to physically start moving Harry away from the robot and down the stairs. "Harry, going on vacation isn't going to kill you."

"Have a great time!" Nancy said, helping escort him toward the door.

Harry was clearly reluctant to leave. He lingered at the door. "Well, I guess I'll send you all a postcard."

They looked at him with mixed wonder and concern. Terry said with sincerity: "Have yourself some fun for a change."

Harry definitely looked like he could use a little fun. He nodded. Then he was out the door.

4

Harry dawdled in the parking lot, checking his luggage. He had his laptop with internal modem so he could at least keep in touch with the volcanology databases while away. And keep tabs on the half dozen restless volcanoes around the world that he knew to be edging toward orange and red on the alert scale.

Harry sighed. No putting it off any longer. He was as ready as he was ever going to be. He slid into his sturdy field vehicle, a 1987 four-wheel-drive Chevy Suburban specially outfitted for a hands-on, off-road geologist. He sorely wished he were on his way to a mission instead of the airport. He pulled the door shut, keyed the ignition, and put the Suburban in reverse. He was backing out when a young assistant volcanologist, Greg Esmail, came running after him.

"Harry—Harry!" he called. "Paul wants to see you

in the lab." Greg was a native Pakistani with wild frizzy hair, dark stubble, and wide eyes that always looked startled; so it was hard for Harry to tell if he was really excited. Even so . . .

"He does?" Harry said, barely able to conceal his own excitement and gratitude—a reprieve! He jammed the truck back into the parking place, killed the engine, and jumped out. Back to work, he hoped. The graph line of Harry's spirits went up in a major spike.

After the disaster in Colombia, Harry had been distraught. He talked about hating volcanoes and everything about them and yet desperately wanted to plunge into work again. Paul Dreyfus, his boss, welcomed him back to work after Marianne's funeral, but resolved to watch him closely. It didn't take Paul long to confirm his fears.

Harry wept behind closed doors, pushed himself insanely, shouted at his colleagues, and broke instruments in his impatience. He wanted to solve the mysteries and danger of volcanoes overnight. He wanted to defang them, emasculate them, analyze them down to molehills. He was out of control.

Paul gently insisted that Harry take a year of paid leave and decompress. Harry didn't fight it. He knew his afterburner was burning too hot. He went docilely.

He put together his hiking and art gear. He laid out an itinerary through Southeast Asia and the island worlds of the South China Sea, where he would walk and paint and lose himself in the study of cultures.

The idyll didn't last long.

Mount Pinatubo in the Philippines started to heat up

just after Harry got to the Far East. Word filtered out from local Aeta tribesmen that small earthquakes were tormenting the land. Harry heard the drum talk eight hundred miles away in the Celebes and made a beeline for the Philippines. When the S.W.A.T. team of U.S. Geological Survey volcanologists arrived with their sophisticated sensing and monitoring equipment, they found that Harry Dalton, supposedly on leave from Cascades Observatory, had been there for days.

Harry, with the equally sophisticated equipment of his experience and senses, already knew the ground underfoot was gravid with magma and ready to give birth. He had visited the headmen in many of the nearby towns and villages and advised them to start getting their people psychologically ready for evacuation—not an easy thing for Filipinos, who are extremely attached to their land.

Over the next forty-five days Harry ran himself ragged doing scut work for the international survey team and personally helping natives in village after village pack up their belongings. When Pinatubo finally blew on June 15, it amounted to a great success for science. Owing to the volcanologists' predictions, eighty-five thousand people had evacuated and been saved.

Thousands of tons of ash and rock cascaded down on empty towns and villages. Tephra and lava bombs barraged the U.S.'s Clark Air Force Base like Zeroes hitting Pearl Harbor, but eighteen thousand servicemen and their dependents had already left. A 130-mile-diameter mushroom cloud spread into the stratosphere and seventy-two hours of total darkness followed, and three hundred people did die. But it could easily have been fifty thousand.

Most of the scientists exulted in the achievement. Harry, however, working himself to a frazzle, brooded. Why did anybody have to die?

When the volcanology teams pulled out, Harry stayed. He donned a cloth face mask, carried an umbrella against the constant ashfall, and lived among the natives. He helped them dig out and rebuild, and get used to wearing shower caps and bandanna masks and live with the intermittent roar of the volcano in the background. He did what he could to prepare them for the lahars to come. And come they did—torrents of hot volcanic muds that arrived with the rainstorms, burying whole villages. Two little girls were buried in the first one, and Harry took it to heart.

He doubled his efforts, working on earth dams, barely sleeping, breathing the dust, eating poorly. Eventually he collapsed.

A palpitating heart, night sweats, disorientation, weight loss and mounting blood pressure—it scared even Harry. He realized he was killing himself, and if he wanted to live, he'd better get out of the volcano business altogether. He faxed his resignation to Paul Dreyfus at Cascades and headed home.

5

"Home" was an apple farm in southeast Washington State where Harry grew up. It was no longer his home, of course, but it was the place it made sense to go to in order to start over after his breakdown at Pinatubo. He went to stay with his widowed mother and put himself through volcano withdrawal.

Had Harry's father still been alive, he wouldn't have gone home under these circumstances. Stern, demanding Dave Dalton had wanted his son to grow up and adopt a "productive" occupation or profession. Apple farming, accounting, doctoring. Hard, honest work that would help keep the world going around and provide a decent living.

Harry had no argument with that. Until a high school science trip to Yellowstone National Park in Wyoming awakened in him a fascination with volcanism. The idea of pounding his tent stakes into a thin crust of earth floating on a sea of 2,000-degree magma the size of Rhode Island was a revelation to a science-minded young boy. And with an eruption cycle of every six hundred thousand years or so, the big Kahuna was due. It would spew ash over a third of the U.S. Harry wanted to know all about it. If it went in his lifetime, he wanted to be there!

Had the father taken the son's sudden passion to become a volcanologist in stride, it might have passed. Instead he condemned it; he wanted no truck with chasing volcanoes. "A waste of time!" he barked. "The damn things are going to spit anyway. You're just trying to avoid hard work."

Harry kept up a running argument trying to convince his father it would be a useful calling. But one day he overheard the old buzzard telling an apple-farming crony, "You don't ever see a son half as good as his father anymore. Not worth a bucket of warm spit as workers. They can't stand it, they fold."

Harry gave up the arguing and got down to the serious business of carving out his own way.

Arriving home from the Philippines, Harry rebuilt his strength, sleeping long hours, eating his mother's cooking, and helping tend the diminished orchards. He got a job substitute teaching at the county central high school and spent his off-hours playing tennis, golfing, and salmon fishing. At night he read fiction, history, biography. Anything but volcanology and the geo sciences.

At five and a half months, he was feeling strong,

healthy, and over his volcano jones—cured. He was about to buy up two neighboring orchards and go into apple farming in a serious way. But the night before he was to make the final offer, he made the mistake of watching a Joseph Campbell television interview about "following your bliss."

He realized instantly and indelibly that apples were not his bliss. Here on the farm he was following nothing, he was running from his true calling.

He showed up at the Cascades Observatory a day later and asked for his old job back. He had prepared a speech about how he had regained his sense of proportion and was prepared to play strictly by the rules. He never got a chance to say it.

Paul Dreyfus welcomed him back to his job the moment he walked through the door. So did the rest of his colleagues. None of them had believed for a minute that Harry was going to be an apple farmer. They had an office pool on the number of weeks or months it would take for him to show his face at the door.

"I gave you six months," Paul said. "So I was off by ten days. Your office is unoccupied. Naturally, I never hired a replacement."

Harry was so touched and relieved he would have kissed every one of them had there not been so much to lose on the macho scale. But they knew from the incandescent smile that broke across his face that the old Harry was back—or would be as soon as he got out in the field and let his stubble grow for a day or three or four.

Now when Harry walked into Paul's office, it was with a look of expectation: One of the Big Fifteen International Decade Volcanoes was threatening probably, and he'd have to drop everything and rush to the site.

Paul was studying some graphs at his desk. He didn't look up, just waved Harry in. "Hi, Harry," he said. "Sit down."

Paul Dreyfus was a rugged outdoor sort, just shy of fifty, a man you would never mistake for a bank teller.

Harry sat, full of anticipation.

"You like hiking in the Cascades, right?" Paul said, looking up.

"Sure," Harry said. "Why?"

"Well—we're picking up some activity around Dante's Peak," Dreyfus said.

Harry laughed, disappointed. "This is a joke, right?" he said. "Dante's Peak?"

Dreyfus handed Harry a paper which contained some infrared satellite images. Harry looked it over.

"Some thermal activity . . . slight temperature changes . . . interesting," Harry said with a smile. "What are the odds of Dante's Peak erupting, a thousand to one?"

"More like ten thousand to one," Paul said.

Terry rushed into Dreyfus's office with some forms for him to sign. "Paul, I need you to—" Seeing Harry, Terry stopped, surprised. "What are you still doing here?" He laid the papers under Dreyfus's eyes. "It's like 'vacation' is a dirty word to him."

"That's *right*," Paul said, sitting back. "Harry, I'm

sorry, I forgot all about it. Hell, I'll find somebody else to go."

Harry stood up and said quickly, "No. No. I'll go. Vacations can wait. This is important."

Paul shook his head and smiled. Suddenly it was important. This was the old Harry, all right. He was glad to see it. Just so he didn't overdo it. But Paul had seen no signs of that since Harry's return.

"Where are you going?" Terry said.

Harry smiled and seemed relieved. "Dante's Peak," he said.

Terry's eyes went wide in disbelief. "Dante's Peak?"

6

Harry headed toward the mountains in his specially
equipped work vehicle—his "hugger orange" GMC
Suburban with the circular USGS emblem on the door.
He cherished this vehicle. He felt confident he could
drive through hell and back in it. It had tubed-steel
brush guards up front protecting four off-road headlights and five more off-road lights up top on a bar. It
had a raised tailpipe and a snorkel into the engine air
intake for going through deep water. For rough terrain
it had wider-than-normal off-road tires and a five-
inch-raised suspension with spacers and heavy-duty
shocks. It also had a power winch, and two antennas
for mobile phone and dispatch radio.

He loved heading into the mountains anywhere, but
he deeply loved the Cascades, the range of mountains
that rumbled the terrain of the whole southeastern

24

quadrant of Washington State. He knew a lot about them, having studied them in person and in books most of his life.

He mulled over what he knew about Dante's Peak as he started to climb the long straightaways and gentle curves of the two-lane blacktop leading up from the coastal plain. He passed Suicide Creek and a big sign by an empty field that read: WORM GROWERS WANTED.

Dante's Peak he had seen only from a distance. It was a snowcapped, pristine, peaceful mountain rising up near the southwestern border of Washington State. It was stunning, but at a mere 9,323 feet, it wasn't by any means the highest peak around. Mount Rainier to the north towered up to 14,411 feet, so high it created its own weather. And nearby Mount St. Helens was a good 300 hundred feet taller until 1980 when it blew its top and lost 1,312 feet in height.

Harry weighed the remote possibilities of real action from Dante's Peak as the road's gentle curves became tighter and he passed Lost Man Creek. The towering pine, cedar, and hemlock forests loomed primevally over the rising roadway. ABRUPT EDGE was a frequent road sign reminder.

Seismic episodes were common occurences throughout the Cascades, Harry was well aware. Underground rumblings were routine—these were geologically young and restless mountains. It was their very seismic aliveness that had led the U.S. Geological Survey to locate its observatory headquarters on the edge of them.

The Cascade Range as a whole, extending its nose up into Canada and its body and tail some six hundred miles all the way down through Oregon into northern

California, was a volcanic crescent. It had been produced by crustal plate subduction activity, the same way the Andes had been. And similarly, activity beginning eons ago was still transforming the landscape today.

But Dante's Peak itself had no modern recorded history of growling or bulging or shaking with mini-quakes, let alone eruptions.

Mount St. Helens, just thirty-three miles away, had erupted spectacularly, to be sure. But it wasn't on the same fault line or considered to be part of the same subterranean magma pipe system. The only way scientists could know anything about Dante's Peak's long-ago spells of activity—prior to the advent of record-keeping man—would be to radiocarbon-date samples of wood and ash deposits buried in the area. But there had been no call—at this one dormant peak among many—to go to all that trouble.

The town of Dante's Peak, population 7,437, was nestled at the foot of the mountain.

It was a jewel of a small town in as scenically beautiful a setting as exists in the continental United States. Hills covered in fir and spruce reached up on all sides, backed by more distant majestic snowy crags—all of them crowned by high white puffy clouds in air so crystal clear you'd think the automobile had never been invented.

There was a fair in progress as Harry's Suburban pulled into town. DANTE'S PEAK PIONEER DAYS FESTIVAL, proclaimed a banner across the main street.

Most of the locals as well as the populace of a good many neighboring towns had turned out. Portable amusement park rides, including a good-sized Ferris

26

wheel, enlivened the town square. The school marching band was coming up Main Street, pumping patri-
otic energy into the popcorn-eating, balloon-clutching
crowd.

Harry rode around the parade, driving slowly down
a parallel street, enjoying the rustic flavor of the place.
Much of its rugged nineteenth-century mining-and-
logging-town personality had been preserved or re-
stored. Two-story frame buildings predominated, with
western-flavored storefronts. Junk-food franchises were
at a minimum, or there in disguise.

Harry drove around until he found his first destina-
tion: Cluster's Last Stand, a wooden lodge-style motel
just across the bridge at one end of town. He pulled in,
and took a walk around to check out the festivities and
the stunning setting of the town, with its evergreen
forests coming right to the edge of civilization.

He saw more banners and balloons, cowboy hats
and straw boaters, a kaleidoscope of colorful garb,
from bold-checked lumberjack shirts to bicycle shorts
to pioneer-style hoedown dresses. The sheriff's depu-
ties on duty actually wore white hats.

A sign in front of Marcy's Cafe & Gas Station said:
EAT HERE, GET GAS. Harry immediately approved of the
burg—a sense of humor along with the feel of a place
people cared about and kept up; here was a community.

He headed back to the motel to get to work.

He stepped inside the piney office and looked around:
framed oil paintings of hunting dogs and bucking bron-
cos and mountain landscapes. A rack of sight-seeing
pamphlets. And the owner, in checked shirt and suspend-

ers, half-glasses, balding, slight frown—Warren Cluster. A lifelong resident of the town, Cluster was a lean cedar tree with none of the bark smoothed off. Pushing sixty, set in his ways, he had an ornery word for almost everyone. He ran off Harry's credit card and shoved the old-fashioned leather-backed register at Harry with a grunt.

Harry signed and Cluster handed him a key. "Room 8," he said with a scowl. "On the corner there."

"Can you tell me where I might find Mayor Wando?" Harry said, hoping not to rile this ill-humored mountain man.

"Yeah," Cluster said, with the first bit of animation he had shown. "She ought to be right around the corner accepting the *Money* magazine award." He drew himself up and went on almost proudly, "Dante's Peak was just named the second most desirable place to live in the United States, population under twenty thousand."

Harry, ever the inquiring scientist, asked the dead-wrong question: "What was number one?"

"I don't know," Cluster said irritably. "Some piece-of-crap town out in Montana—who cares."

Harry was sorry he asked. He took his key and went to stow his things in his cabin, making a mental note to show enthusiasm for this town the next time he talked to a resident.

7

Rachel Wando was running late, not exactly a "stop the presses" situation. She had too many things to do, too many places to be, too many people to please. As is often the case with single parents.

She was dashing around her upstairs bedroom, half dressed in a nice suit, heels, pearl drop earrings—frantically looking for some missing thing as she raced to get ready.

Rachel was in her mid-thirties, and genuinely unaware of just how pretty she was. Wonderful bones, strong, elegant jawline, chameleon eyes that could look sleepily humorous or spitfire bright depending on the needs of the moment. She wore her light ash brown hair at a shaggy shoulder length and was forever throwing it out of her eyes like a mop. Not much of her time went into worrying over her appearance. She was ordinary looking in every way, she assumed, and at this moment as all others, would have been much more comfortable in jeans and a flannel shirt.

She muttered to herself, practicing a speech as she passed through her cluttered den/office, still looking for the missing something. "Ladies and gentlemen," she intoned. "I'd like to thank Karen from *Money* magazine for . . ." She stopped, sighed in exasperation. "What is it? 'Karen' or 'Kathy'?"

Rachel's ten-year-old daughter, Lauren, followed her mother around, coaching her from a copy of the text in her hands. Lauren was beautiful, a smaller, dark-eyed version of her mother. "It's Karen, Mom," she said. "Karen. For the tenth time, Karen. And you're going to be late."

"Have you seen my good jacket?" Rachel said finally. She hated to admit being this disorganized to one of her kids, whom she was constantly hounding to get it together.

"You don't have a good jacket," Lauren said.

"The blue one," Rachel said with a give-me-a-break look.

"It's on the back of the chair in the kitchen," Lauren said. "Hurry up, Mom."

Rachel stormed down the stairs, Lauren right at her heels. She ran into the kitchen, grabbed up the jacket, threw it on, and ran down the hall to her son's bedroom. She banged on the door.

"Graham," she called, "it's time to go."

No response from inside. Rachel flung open the door to a typical teenager's room. Pictures of Kurt

Cobain on the wall, a Smashing Pumpkins poster. The room was empty of teenager, however.

"Where's your brother?" Rachel said.

"He said he'll meet us there," Lauren said. "Let's go, you'll be late." She grabbed her mother's hand and pulled her out the front door.

They shot out of the house and into Rachel's Land Cruiser. The pale blue truck screeched away down the street, got on a main road, turned up onto the bridge, and sped across it into the town's commercial thoroughfare.

One of the first businesses they passed was the Blue Moon Cafe on the corner. Rachel's place of business. It had a CLOSED sign in the window.

Most other shops were closed and there were few people on the main drag. Almost everybody was already where Rachel was supposed to be. A town with high civic pride it was, thanks in part to Rachel's efforts in the eight years she'd been mayor.

She turned off onto Chelan Street and looked for a parking place in front of Dante's Peak High School.

No room. Oh, the hell with it, I'm the mayor, she thought. She double-parked the Land Cruiser, blocking in another vehicle, and she and Lauren made a dash toward the crowd gathered in the schoolyard.

At the far end of the yard, the high school band was running through its Sousa and fight-song repertoires. Up on the stage local business leader Les Worrell, the bald-pated, paunchy hardware store owner with the potato nose, craned his neck looking for the tardy mayor.

Some Pioneer Days citizens in old-time costumes

decorated the stage with their presence. There were a preacherman with black hat, an aproned pioneer wife, schoolgirls in pigtails and white gloves, a frontier businessman with flowing Buffalo Bill hair. They all stood dutifully waiting, exchanging remarks with the crowd.

Harry was there too, standing at the front of the audience, looking as bored and impatient as Les and everybody else.

Everybody else but one.

Sitting near Les on the stage, holding a plaque, was Karen Narlington from the San Francisco bureau of *Money* magazine. She was an attractive, slightly brittle blonde in a power suit and her hair up in a chic chignon, early to middle thirties. Ironically, it was this obvious dynamo who seemed the most relaxed person present, smiling placidly and gazing around at the scenery, blithely undisturbed by the delay.

After all, its leisurely pace of life was one of the reasons Dante's Peak was receiving this award today. Truth be told, Ms. Narlington was picturing herself in a granny dress and Birkenstocks making bread in her own shop down there on Main Street. The delicious aroma would bring in customers and neighbors from the street. She would know everybody. By and by all the strapping, eligible, supremely stalwart young mountain men would find their way to her door and she could have her pick . . .

Les gave a relieved sigh as Rachel and Lauren came into view. "It's about time," he said half out loud. He signaled to the bandleader, who quickly brought the fourth rendition of the school fight song to a halt.

Karen snapped out of it and put on her crisp power smile as Les moved to the microphone and began the proceedings.

"Ladies and gentlemen," he said. "I'd like to welcome the mayor of Dante's Peak, Rachel Wando."

There was applause as Rachel ran up onto the stage straightening her jacket, trying to look dignified.

Harry's brows lifted. Mayor Wando was not what he'd expected.

"Today is a very special day in Dante's Peak," Les went on, "and to kick off the proceedings, I'd like to introduce Karen Narlington from *Money* magazine."

Karen stepped forward with her plaque and flashed a beautiful bonded-teeth smile. Her designer outfit— her sheer urban chicness—stood out in this rustic setting. She was a knockout; she had all the townswomen staring at her in silent envy.

But Harry didn't notice. He had eyes only for this interesting-looking mayor who now followed Karen to the podium. Then he caught himself and shook his head in mild surprise. He didn't look at women, not since Marianne.

"Thank you very much, Les," Karen said. "Mayor Wando, it gives me great pleasure to present to you a *Money* magazine award. Dante's Peak—the second most desirable place to live in the United States, population under twenty thousand."

The proud citizenry applauded and cheered. Rachel moved forward to the microphone, making a quick search of her pockets for something—her speech. It was gone. She smiled to the crowd and improvised.

"Thank you, Ka—" She stopped herself, unsure of

33

the name. Then plunged ahead. "Thank you, Kathy," she said confidently.

Lauren, standing a few feet to the right of Harry, called out: "It's Karen."

The whole crowd burst into laughter, including Harry.

Rachel hid her embarrassment behind a valiant smile and pushed on. "This award means a lot to us," she said. "We've always been very proud of our town. It's beautiful, safe, and a wonderful place to raise a family. And now with—"

Cheers and applause interrupted her. She stopped and let the town exult.

"And now with the prospect of a major investment in our economic future by Elliot Blair of Blair Industries . . ." She paused and gestured. "Mr. Blair, would you stand up, please."

A young businessman in cashmere blazer and slacks rose from his seat on the stage and held up his hand to acknowledge the town's applause. The handsome, prosperous-looking Elliot Blair. Les beamed at him. Rachel too applauded.

"Next year," she said when the applause died down, "we're going to be number one."

A downright raucous salvo of yelling and clapping from the happy, hopeful crowd.

8

The landscape rose gradually at first, then steeply behind the town in the direction of the mountain. Several blacktopped county roads led into the craggy forested backcountry. Some folks lived up that way on the ridges, but not many. Forestry Service rangers patrolled the territory regularly in daylight. Serious hikers drove up there to the trailheads at the base of the mountain.

Young people with beer-drinking, sex, and skinny-dipping on their minds knew the mountainside well. It was a rite of passage to learn and navigate all the hidden turnoffs, dirt spurs, and grown-over fire roads leading away to the myriad streams and little lakes dotting the flanks and hollows of the peak. Deliciously private, sylvan spots they were—spots that would live forever in their minds as the settings for first love and forbidden pleasures.

One spot for trysts and skinny-dipping that lured certain of the locals was doubly attractive because it was officially forbidden. Twonset Hot Springs it was called. NO BATHING, said the sign posted at the edge of the water.

But its mossy, ferny banks and leafy overhangs of big-leaf maples and red cedar trees were too enticing. On cool summer nights, when the bubbling water and steam rising from the pool offered sensual refuge from the chill in the air, it was impossible to resist.

Some locals even went for it in the heat of the day. And some down-mountain types—tourists—stumbling upon it by accident, thought a short dip couldn't hurt and would probably be salubrious. Almost always, they were right.

On this afternoon when Rachel was busy speaking to the townsfolk about how blessed they were to reside in Eden, a draped T-shirt obscured the NO BATHING sign at Twonset Hot Springs, and more clothes were piled around it.

A young man and woman, visitors to the area, were about to flaunt the warning.

The young guy had read the message, smiled, and stripped off his things, then he tossed them at the sign. His girlfriend, in her mid-twenties, had laughingly stripped off her mini-tee and bra and shorts and was only a step behind him as he approached the steaming water.

The man stepped naked into the hot water and

waded out. A moment later the woman dipped a toe in to join him.

"Ow!" she said. "It's really hot."

"Hmm," the man said, "do you think maybe that's why they call it the Twonset Hot Springs?"

She waded in and splashed him. He splashed her. They eased down into the steaming water and relaxed, taking in the scenery. The man filled his lungs with clean fresh air.

"Is this great or what?" he said, watching two Steller's jays bickering noisily in one of the cedar trees. Overhead, a brace of red-tailed hawks sailed lazily by, scanning the alpine meadows above for signs of a meal—rabbits, nutrias, wood rats, ground squirrels.

"It sure beats the hell out of Los Angeles," the woman said. She gasped and pointed: A white-tailed deer was standing like a statue back in the woods, looking at them. He sniffed the air and disappeared like a ghost in the blink of an eye. A harbinger of some sort, she thought.

"Maybe we should move here," the man said. He was a lean, muscled sort. He looked like he could adapt to mountain life.

"I'd go nuts in a week," the woman said with a laugh.

A sizable splash behind them. Then a rustle in the bushes. They looked around and saw nothing. They were both quiet for a moment, listening.

"It's okay," said the guy. "Some animal."

But he didn't sound quite sure of that. What animal or bird would be plunging into water like this? It was neither drinkable nor a home for prey. He tried to take things back to normal with a smile. "Come here, gorgeous," he said, stretching out a hand.

She bestirred herself and started across the bubbling pool toward him.

A loud cracking sound.

The ground around them gave a shake.

The woman looked at the man, frightened. "Jerry—" she said, her voice shaky.

As she spoke, a flock of spotted owls fluttered up from their daytime sleep back in the old-growth spruce. Black and white magpies took noisy flight from the bushes bordering the pool. The man and woman turned to look at the birds. At the far side of the pool, gravel fell. The ground shook harder.

The woman moved faster toward the man, terrified. Then she screamed.

At her feet, the rocks on the bottom of the hot springs shifted. Large bubbles rose around the woman and steam enveloped her. She yelled out in pain. "Oh my God it's hot!"

She screamed again, and the scream carried down the mountain.

9

At Dante's Peak High School, Rachel wound up her speech. She thanked Karen and *Money* magazine again and brought the proceedings to a close, to a final burst of applause from the happy crowd.

Rachel followed the rest of the town notables down off the stage. She moved through the crowd toward her daughter, and found herself face to face with the dark-eyed stranger who had been waiting impatiently to meet her.

"Hi, I'm Harry Dalton," he said, sticking his hand out. "With the U.S. Geological Survey, and—"

He was interrupted by Les Worrell and Elliot Blair, both charging at Rachel, beaming.

"Wonderful speech, Rachel," Les said. "Really inspiring, right, Elliot?"

It came to Rachel in a rush who this Harry was. Not

a good mix, she instantly realized—the Geological Survey volcano guy and the would-be investor in the town. What's a volcano scientist doing in the country's second-most desirable town under twenty thousand? But she had to be polite.

"You've got a way with words," Blair said to her with a warm smile and a lasting handshake. He was a early-middle-aged go-getter, self-confident and sleek as a seal.

"That's very nice of you, Mr. Blair," Rachel said with her most politic smile, "and I—"

Harry had dillydallied long enough, he wanted to get going. He moved to cut in front of these doofuses. "Um . . . excuse me, Mayor Wando, gentlemen," he said.

"And you are . . . ?" Blair said.

"I'm Harry Dalton," he said peremptorily, "from—"

Rachel quickly blurted, "From Portland. Right? Your boss, Mr. Driscoll—"

"It's Dreyfus," Harry said.

"Right," Rachel said. "He told me you were coming—he asked me to show you around." She turned to Les and Blair. "Bye now."

Rachel took Harry's arm and hustled him off.

Lauren caught up and checked out this guy her mom was leading away. "Good job, Mom," she said after giving Harry the once-over.

"Where's your brother?" Rachel said, dropping Harry's arm and pushing Lauren's hair out of her face.

Lauren hesitated a beat, looking a little guilty. "I don't know, Mom," she said. Which was a white lie at best.

"Never mind," Rachel said, irritated. "I know where he is."

Rachel grabbed Lauren's hand and began pulling her off in the direction of the Land Cruiser. Harry followed. Now he was beginning to feel a little testy.

They got to Rachel's Land Cruiser where Mr. Gunn, the owner of the car Rachel had blocked by double-parking, was waiting, angry.

"This is not the way to get reelected, Mayor Wando," Mr. Gunn grumbled sarcastically.

"Sorry, Mr. Gunn," Rachel said, fumbling for her keys. She dropped them, picked them up, unlocked the doors, and nudged Lauren hurriedly into the backseat. She turned to Harry. "Get in," she said with a big bright smile. "I have to make a stop along the way."

Harry marveled at how this woman managed to charm people even while fumbling and delaying.

They all piled in the Land Cruiser.

They drove through town and immediately turned off onto a county road leading toward the backcountry. Rachel chattered with some enthusiasm about the plans Elliot Blair had for the area, the first of which was a combination ski-summer conference resort on the lower western slopes of Dante's Peak. The jobs that would come with the resort were very much needed to replace those being lost in the diminishing mining and logging industries. Rachel rattled on about how especially gratified she was that Blair seemed equal parts entrepreneur and environmentalist—that he in fact spent far more time talking about preserving the scenic wonders of the place than about making money.

Harry, plenty sick of this claptrap about the businessman-saint, broke in: "Where are we going?" He couldn't keep the slight edge out of his voice.

"We're there," Rachel said, lighting up her face with her friendliest smile. She veered off the county road onto a rutted track running back among the tall firs. Abruptly they came to an abandoned silver mine in the face of a mountainside. Rachel pulled up in front of the corroded metal gates.

Big red and white signs said NO TRESPASSING and KEEP OUT.

Behind the broken-down chain-link fence, the gated mine entrance had plainly been breached. The metal sheeting had been bent up at one of the bottom corners to make a crawl space.

Rachel was peeved. She leaned on the horn. They waited. Again: HONK!

"Do you have any kids?" Lauren said casually to Harry.

"Uh, no, I don't," he said distractedly. He had work to do. This was no fun for him.

"You're lucky," Lauren said, all bright-eyed innocence. "Right, Mom?"

Rachel smiled. "Some days, you kids can be just great," she said. She stared at the mine entrance impatiently. Still no movement from inside. The smile left her face. She got out of the truck.

"And *other* days . . . ," she muttered, and stalked around to the fence. She stepped through and walked around a pile of mine tailings to the sheet-metal doors, she leaned down to the opening and shouted. "Graham! . . . Graham!"

Still no response.

Back in the truck, Lauren watched, uncomfortable. "My brother Graham's in a lot of trouble," she said to Harry.

"He is?" Harry said. He liked this little girl's concern and loyalty for her brother.

From out of the mine came three fourteen-year-old boys, Graham and two of his buddies, Tom and Mark. Graham was a lean-built, floppy-haired kid with big dark eyes that didn't miss much. Floppy jeans and a checked flannel shirt like his buddies. They were all covered in mine dust.

Rachel was furious. "You two go home," she said to Tom and Mark. "You," she said to Graham, "get in the truck."

The two boys ran off. Graham stood for a moment. At fourteen, Graham was half-man and half-boy and not comfortable being either. Rachel pushed him toward the truck. He moved without looking at her. He shot one glance at Harry—Who the hell are you?—as he got into the truck.

Rachel slammed in behind the wheel and cranked the truck into a U-turn. "I don't know what's wrong with you," she said as she bounced the truck out the rutted lane toward the road.

"Can we do this some other time?" Graham said in his bored teenager tones.

Rachel wrenched the truck onto the macadam road to town and rolled her eyes. How many times had she had to make this speech? "The mine is dangerous," she said, affecting calm. "That's why it's off-limits. Mothers are supposed to stop their children from getting hurt. God knows why."

Graham gave Harry a sideways look, embarrassed by his mother. Harry gave him back a grin of complicity. It seemed to help.

10

At one of the town's three stoplights, Rachel leaned out the window of the Land Cruiser and spoke to a middle-aged blonde woman she saw on the street—Dr. Jane Fox.

"Dr. Fox," she said, "I hear Mrs. Mackey was sick."

"Just a touch of the flu," Dr. Fox said. Then, looking more closely into the truck, she saw the strange man in there. "How are you, Rachel?" she asked pointedly.

Rachel recognized Dr. Fox's interest and reacted quickly, lest the wrong idea get around. "This is Dr. Dalton from the United States Geological Survey," she said.

"How do you do?" Harry called over with a polite half smile.

Dr. Fox looked Harry over, obviously unconvinced that this was all just official business. She opened her mouth to probe further, but the light changed. Rachel took off in a hurry.

Dr. Fox watched her go.

Rachel was Dante's Peak's most eligible single woman, motherhood notwithstanding, in the opinion of Dr. Fox, who had been working for several years to get her hooked up with the right man. She had gone so far as to invite the stockbroker son of a former medical colleague in Seattle to come visit for a weekend. It looked promising—at least Rachel sat through dinner and made pleasant conversation with him. Then they walked out on Fox's deck after dinner and the man started sneezing. He was allergic to the oil in pine needles, it turned out. He left the same night.

Several other friends had engineered fix-ups, and Rachel had dutifully endured the agony-filled dates. One was a neat freak who actually shuddered at the state of Rachel's house and offered to polish the bottoms of her copper pots for her. Two men in a row were so obsessed with their own needs that it was clear after ten minutes they were looking for mothers. Rachel had enough kids, thank you very much.

The last fix-up blind date she'd gone out with had seemed a nice enough fellow—he was a freelance book editor—but he absolutely could not make eye contact with her. Whoa. What was going on there?

Thereafter, Rachel kindly but firmly declined all fix-up offers and made it known she was not on the market.

Dr. Fox, though, had not given up. Rachel was too smart and attractive and full of love to go through the rest of her life without a good man. Dr. Fox had met a

46

professional golfer named Peter Lantana on a flight from Los Angeles. He was just getting a divorce. She'd invited him to come spend a few days once the pro golf season was over this fall. She hadn't told Rachel yet.

11

At last they were on their way up the mountain. Rachel powered the Land Cruiser confidently around the curves of the two-lane. Harry sat beside her. In the backseat were Graham and Lauren. Nobody was talking.

Graham was looking out the window and digging in his pocket at the same time. He took out a quartz crystal he had found in the mine and held it up to the window. The sunlight refracted into all the colors of the spectrum.

"It looks like a rainbow," Lauren said.

"Can I have a look at that?" Harry said.

Graham passed it up for Harry to see.

Harry turned it over, examined it. "This is a smoky quartz crystal," he said. "You can see the silica's taken in some gas, giving it that smoky look." He passed the crystal back to Graham.

"You know about this stuff?" Lauren said, interested. Science was her favorite course at school.

"Dr. Dalton is a geologist," Rachel said.

"Volcanologist, actually," Harry said.

Lauren hesitated. "You mean like Dr. Spock?" she said.

"It's *Mr.* Spock," Graham said, with all the condescension due a ten-year-old.

Harry laughed.

"Hey, Mom," Graham said. "Drop me off at Grandma's."

"Yeah! Me too," Lauren said, excited.

"You're not tagging along," Graham sneered.

"I can do what I want," Lauren said.

A brawl started up between the two—pushing and yelling.

That was enough for Rachel. She said sharply: "Don't start fighting! Nobody's going."

Her sharp tone got the kids' attention. Harry's, too. Tough, he thought. In command.

"I've kept Dr. Dalton waiting long enough," she said.

"Please?" Lauren said, sweet and winning. She had begging down to an art. Harry smiled, looked to Rachel. "If you'd like to drop them off at your mother's place I really don't mind. "

Your mother's place . . . The kids snickered at that. Harry didn't get why, but he saw it made Rachel burn.

"She's not my mother, she's my mother-in-law,"

49

Rachel said, throwing the hair out of her eyes in irritation. "Make that ex-mother-in-law."

Whew, thought Harry. Dangerous seismic activity there.

12

Mirror Lake was a high, pristine body of mountain water shimmering in the afternoon sun. On a mid-level flank of Dante's Peak, it was fed by a number of streams that were fed by snowmelt from the year-round icecap on the peak above.

Harry admired the dormant volcano's near-perfect cone shape from the truck as Rachel pulled off the two-lane onto a long dirt driveway.

Dante's Peak was, as advertised, a scenic marvel. Harry knew it to be a perennial favorite of hikers, climbers, snowshoers, and cross-country skiers, who referred to it as a sleeping beauty. Mule deer and elk grazed on its lower slopes and shared the alpine meadows with black bears and grouse and ptarmigan. Higher up, bald eagles patrolled and mountain goats tried to stay above the hunting range of cougars and gray wolves.

Rachel's truck rolled down the dirt road and came out on the shore of the lake. It was an achingly beautiful spot, with the high floating clouds and the magnificent snowy peak mirrored in the glassy water.

Rachel drove toward a small log lodge nestled in a cove where the surrounding woods crowded down to the shore of the lake.

Across the lake on one side, the virgin spruce, Douglas fir, and hemlock marched up a steep mountainside marked by sharp ravines and firebreaks.

On the other side, the lake seemed to end in the air where the mountain fell away below.

As the Land Cruiser drove up, it was met by a skinny, barking runt of a dog. It was Roughy, who ran alongside the truck, trying both to bark and hold on to the old shoe dangling from her mouth. The kids adored her. Lauren cried out, "Hi, Roughy!"

Rachel parked the truck and they all piled out.

"Give me that, Roughy," Graham said, grabbing one end of the shoe, wrestling with the dog for it. The boy got it and ran on the grass and threw it into the woods. Roughy scampered off after it.

Harry could see that Rachel clearly didn't want to be here. He took in the handsome lodge of cut cedar logs, noted its wraparound plank porch and log railings. "What a great spot," he said almost to himself.

Lauren ran toward the lodge calling, "Hey, Grandma! Where are you?"

An attractive older woman appeared from behind the dwelling with a big smile on her face. Ruth, Rachel's former mother-in-law, was a high-spirited, independent-minded woman determined not to give in to age. She wore her hair in a stylishly short coif. She was dressed in jeans and a hand-knit Indian-design vest over a Pendleton work shirt.

"Well, look who's here," she said, opening her arms to Lauren.

Lauren ran into her arms and they hugged. Graham came over, too, and gave her a big hug. Both were obviously crazy about their grandma.

Rachel and Ruth looked at each other. No love lost there.

"Hello, Ruth," Rachel managed.

Ruth nodded ever so slightly, but was more interested in giving the new man the once-over. "Hi, Rachel," she said, all the while looking at Harry. "You Rachel's boyfriend?"

"No," Harry said. He was getting used to this drill. "I'm Harry Dalton with the United States Geological Survey. I'm here to look over your mountain."

"Bunch of you people came up here right after Mount St. Helens went nuts back in 1980," Ruth said. "There was nothing going on then—there's nothing going on here now."

Harry smiled at Ruth's straightforward style.

"I'm gonna take Dr. Dalton up to the high lake," Rachel said. "Is it okay if the kids stay here?"

"Sure. But why don't we all go?" Ruth said. She smelled adventure.

Rachel shot a dubious look in the direction of her kids. "Um," she said, "They—"

But Ruth had already decided. She said to the kids

excitedly, "We can go swimming and mess around in the hot springs on the way back. How about it, kids?" Harry figured this was Ruth's style—plunge ahead like a fullback regardless of others' needs or reservations. He could see where some of the trouble between these two came from. But he suspected that was only part of it.

"Yeah!" Graham said, punching the air. He was on board. "Our swim stuff's in the truck."

The kids and Ruth headed off toward the truck. Rachel just stood there pissed.

Harry smiled. "Shall we?" he said. He was getting interested in the dynamics of this little family despite himself. These two women were like scorpions in a bottle.

Rachel stormed off toward the truck. Harry followed.

13

Deeper into the graduated slope of Dante's Peak, Rachel maneuvered the Land Cruiser up a rocky road full of switchbacks and sheer falls first on one side, then the other. The kids leaned out the windows right along with Roughy, stoked on the spectacular views and the slight whiff of danger from the narrow winding road.

Rachel horsed the truck up and over the shoulder of a ridge and down to the edge of the high lake. Much smaller than Mirror Lake by the lodge below, it sat in the crater formed on the side of the mountain by an ancient spur eruption. There was a deep, almost unnaturally blue tint to the ice-cold water, the result of gases fed into the lake from the volcanic bed below.

Ruth, the kids, and Roughy ran along the edge and up a slope. They messed around on the hill, yelling and throwing rocks into the lake, while Harry went to work below.

Rachel watched as Harry knelt by the lake with a digital pH meter.

"What are you doing?" she asked.

"Checking the acidity of the water," Harry said.

"Like a pool man?" she said

Harry grinned good-naturedly. "Exactly," he said. "Like a pool man." He removed the meter and stood up, glancing at Rachel. "They'll check this pH reading against samples they took fifteen years ago."

"From here?" she said.

"Yep," he said. "And from Mount St. Helens. They made baseline measurements throughout this whole section of the Cascades at that time. You are one big laboratory for volcanism. You should feel privileged." He said it with a grin.

Rachel gave a dubious look back. A scream of delight drew her attention to Ruth and the kids fooling around on the hill. She seemed both irritated and a bit sad.

Harry looked at the meter reading. He was surprised at what it said. He touched the water dripping from the meter. It stung the skin of his fingers. Now he was definitely concerned.

He raised his head, changed his focus from near to far, and scanned the forest coming down to the edge of the water. Of the pine trees on the far bank of the lake, most looked healthy. But a handful right along the bank had toppled over, their branches stripped of growth.

"Those dead trees," he said to Rachel. "Any idea how long ago they died?"

Rachel, still watching the kids and Ruth, was distracted. "I'm sorry?" she said.

Harry pointed across the lake. "Any idea when those trees died?" he said.

Rachel looked at the trees, noticing them for the first time, and shrugged. Across the lake the other way, the outside of the crater cut steeply down the mountain. The trees along that edge looked healthy.

"Could have been the winter storms, I suppose," she said. "Why? Do you think we have a problem?"

"I go out on twenty-five, thirty calls like this a year," Harry said, making some entries in a small notebook. "Ninety-eight percent of them are false alarms."

"What about the other two percent?" Rachel said, finally focusing on what Harry was saying.

He gave a little shake of his head. "You wouldn't have to worry about moving up on that 'best places to live' list."

Rachel gave him a jaundiced look.

He moved off by himself along the wooded bank, looking for other dying vegetation or marine animals. Such dying-off he knew, could be a sign of unusual levels of carbon dioxide being released from the depths of the lake by seismic activity.

Carbon dioxide was a red flag to a volcanologist. Ubiquitous in the atmosphere and a normal component of animal respiration and metabolism, it was lethal in large amounts. It formed carbonic acid in the blood, causing acidosis, which could kill. In the soil, too much carbon dioxide asphyxiated oxygen-loving tree and plant roots the same way it did animals and humans. Harry made a note to bring an instrument for testing soil gases the next time he came.

He further scanned the scene: Some floating fish and farther out some dead water weeds came into view. Along the shore, more fir trees in early stages of decline. He crouched and examined an exposed bank. No sign of burrowing animals or insect life. To Harry these absences were indications of possible carbon dioxide release from volcanic activity. But not proof. Not enough to be at all sure. And yet . . .

Looking into the deep blue waters of the little lake, he flashed on the strangest, deadliest instance of carbon dioxide upwelling in recent times, in a beautiful, harmless-looking blue lake just like this one.

It was ten years ago at Lake Nyos in northwestern Cameroon in Africa, a lovely blue crater lake. It seemed that heavily gas-saturated bottom water, undisturbed for eons, was jolted by a small volcanic quake. The cold water rose off the bottom, and as it did, carbon dioxide released from high pressure formed bubbles that then surged upward in a chimneylike column. The gaseous foam burst through the surface in an unbelievable fountain five hundred feet high. A deadly mist enveloped the entire lake and surrounding landscape, instantly killing more than a thousand people and all the cattle and other animals. There were so few survivors it was weeks before word of the tragedy filtered out from the remote area.

Closer to home just last winter, Harry recollected a weird instance of a forest ranger running into a carbon dioxide booby trap on patrol in the backcountry. At

Mammoth Mountain in central California, in the Long Valley caldera—a sprawling, much-studied volcano system that has been geologically active for four million years—the bespectacled, somewhat tubby forest ranger was trying to escape a heavy snowstorm in a cabin that was nearly buried in snow. He climbed in through a trapdoor near the roof and clambered down inside. He couldn't catch his breath. His pulse went up to 200. He started seeing stars. He just barely managed to climb up, throw himself half over the high threshold, and hang there breathing as hard as he could for the many minutes it took him to recover.

It was a carbon dioxide tiger trap. The colorless, odorless, heavier-than-air gas seeped out of the ground from the volcano hidden below and collected near the floor of the cabin, held in by the insulation of snow. Another few whiffs and the ranger would have died on the spot.

Harry looked over and saw Rachel playing with her kids. These were stories he decided, it would not be necessary to tell her at this time. He headed back to the truck.

14

Back at a lower altitude, Rachel steered the Land Cruiser off the mountain road onto a turnout. Behind her the kids were bouncing on the seat waiting for the truck to stop. This was one of their all-time favorite places—a little spooky and mysterious, a hint of danger, rarely visited. Delicious.

The truck came to a halt and everyone tumbled out, dog first. A path led off the road through the tall trees. The kids arrowed straight for it, rushing with their bathing suits toward the forbidden hot springs, accompanied by the bounding Roughy.

"Last one in's a wienie head!" Lauren called.

Rachel yelled after them, "Watch out for poison oak when you're putting your suits on . . . And *wait for me* before going in!"

The kids were already too far down the path to hear

her. For some reason this place always made Rachel a little bit nervous.

But not Ruth.

"They'll be fine," she said. "Hey, wait up!" She took off down the path after the kids, toward the hot springs.

Rachel shook her head, then noticed Harry gazing at a dramatic igneous rock formation by the side of the road. "A man who stares at a rock has either a lot on his mind," she said, "or nothing."

Harry laughed. "The rocks up there give us some idea of the last time this area was active."

"Which was when?" Rachel said.

"About seven thousand years ago," Harry said, walking to the edge of the road and looking down. He could see parts of the town far below.

"Hmmm," Rachel said, relieved to hear it, "as recent as that . . ."

At that moment, a horrifying sound came ripping through the trees from the direction of the hot springs: Lauren screaming in anguish!

Harry and Rachel took off running down the path and through the overgrowth toward the sound. Rachel's heart was pounding out of her chest.

They burst into the clearing.

Lauren stood there fully clothed, staring at something, an anguished look on her face. Graham moved up beside her and looked. His face twisted a little too.

Rachel and Harry ran to them, stopped, stared down: two dead squirrels. Using a stick, Graham flipped one of them over.

"Oooh. Don't touch it," Lauren said with a shudder.

It was a pretty graphic sight, the squirrels were covered with maggots.

"Yech," Rachel said, turning her head away.

Ruth peered at the squirrel with clinical interest. Death held no threat for her. "Must be some sort of squirrel epidemic," she said. "They're dropping like that all over the mountain."

Harry's antennae twitched. He bent to examine the squirrels more closely. Once again he had to conceal his concern.

The kids, tired of the sight, moved off toward the hot springs.

"I found Roughy near here," Ruth said. "Six years ago. She'd had a fight with a porcupine. Saddest sight I've ever seen."

Rachel couldn't find it in her to empathize; she walked away.

Harry, though, smiled. He sort of liked the old girl—liked her spirit. "You'd never know it to look at her now," he said. "Little beauty."

Ruth smiled as Harry gave the dog a pat.

15

Lauren and Graham approached the edge of the hot springs, their suits in their arms. They stared at the eerie scene with a little awe.

"This is *so cool*," Lauren said low.

There was so much steam rising from the surface of the springs that it obscured whatever might have been floating out in the middle of the water. Dead silence enveloped the pool—none of the usual bird and animal noises. A streamer of moss dropped from an overhanging tree and hit the water with a soft splash.

Then a bubbling sound, and a wave of sulfur dioxide and other smelly gases rose up with the steam.

"Phew! It stinks," Graham said. "I don't know if I want to go in."

"It smells like your room," Lauren said. "You go in *there*."

She turned to go into the bushes to change.

If she was going in, Graham sure wasn't going to flake.

Both kids changed in the bushes. Lauren, stepping out in her little one-piece, pointed to the T-shirt draped across the NO BATHING sign.

"Look! . . . Grandma!" she called.

Ruth came over, picked up the T-shirt, and looked around. She saw the two sets of clothes. Curious, she turned toward the steam-shrouded pool and moved forward to the bank. She peered through the miasma, looking to see if there was anybody out there. She called out tentatively: "Hello? Anyone here?"

Harry and Rachel caught up.

"Sometimes couples come sneaking up here for a hot dip and some hot nooky," Ruth said.

"Ruth!" Rachel said.

Ruth waved away her concern. "For God sakes, Rachel," she said.

By now Graham had changed into his baggy bathing suit. He was climbing onto a little overhang and getting ready to do a cannonball into the water. He screwed up his nose at the rotten-egg smell and approached the edge.

Harry looked at the hot springs. A horrible thought crossed his mind. He went into action even as he shouted: "Stay back from the water!" He sprinted and made a leaping dive, grabbing Graham in a flying tackle around the waist just as the boy was leaning forward to cannonball into the water. Graham and Harry landed in a rolling heap at the water's edge.

Lauren, down the bank, let out a small squeak of alarm and stepped back.

"What the hell—?" Ruth said.

Before Harry could launch into an explanation, Lauren let go with a real scream.

Some steam had moved off, and there, floating facedown, horribly burned, was the body of the young woman tourist.

In an instant Graham was there at her side, gaping at the parboiled blistered form.

Rachel ran to her children, both of them staring fixedly at the body—hypnotized by their first look at death. Rachel led them gently away; they could not take their eyes off the body even as they went.

Harry looked at the lifeless woman. And altogether unbidden, the memory of another time, another place, swept over him. Another tragic, needless, stupid death. And then he had to turn away. And walk off into the woods by himself.

16

Men from the local hospital enclosed the corpses in zippered rubber body bags, an appalling end to what had begun as an innocent mountain idyll. The EMTs carried the bodies on stretchers along the winding sylvan path out to the road.

There they loaded them into the ambulance that was pulled at an angle into the turnout, next to a police car with its bubble flashing red and blue.

Harry stood with his back to the goings-on, looking at the town of Dante's Peak below. He was having a conversation on his cell phone.

". . . Paul, I think we should monitor the entire area," Harry said. "Get the whole shooting match in here—seismometers, temp gauges, tilt and deformation sensors, gas analyzers. We should wire the whole mountain, not take a chance."

He listened to Paul's response, then went on. "No, no visible plume, and I know it all costs—"

He listened again.

"I don't know," he continued, "but the acidity in the lake is high enough to bother me, and there's enough carbon dioxide coming out of the soil to have started killing trees and wildlife. I recommend at least a Level D."

A Level D status report, indicating "moderate unrest," was the fourth lowest of five levels of seriousness on the international volcano warning scale.

Paul hastened to remind Harry that even a lowly Level D was usually not called unless the region experienced a swarm of small earthquakes—a hundred or more, or two magnitude 3.0 quakes or greater—in one day. Paul also reminded Harry how the news media consistently and maddeningly failed to distinguish between low-level status reports and high-level volcano alerts, reporting any warning as an imminent threat to life and limb. No need to invite that, he added.

Unsaid, but at the back of Paul's mind, was his uncertainty even now about Harry's judgment in a case like this. Harry was not the same cold-eyed, coolly objective scientist he once was, Dreyfus feared. How could he be? How much was he reading into the present situation? How much was he trying to recapture the past, but to do it right this time, to play it extra safe?

In short, Dreyfus suspected Harry of wanting to release the doves much too early, and he was listening closely to everything Harry said in order to make a sound judgment.

At the other end of the turnout, Ruth was now in the driver's seat of Rachel's truck. Rachel stood outside the Land Cruiser on the roadway hugging each of her kids. "You guys okay?" she said, wiping away the remaining tears of fright and dismay that had flowed from Lauren's eyes when the reality had sunk in.

The kids nodded they were okay.

"I love you," Rachel said quietly and reassuringly. They hugged their mother again, then hopped into the truck.

Rachel put a hand on the truck door and nodded to Ruth. "I shouldn't be too long," she said.

Ruth jerked the truck into gear, all businesslike, and drove off.

Rachel, putting on her civic-responsibility hat, hurried over to Harry just as he was hanging up the phone.

"Any idea who they were?" Harry asked, watching the ambulance with the two bodies pull slowly away.

"Nobody I know. Probably tourists," Rachel said. They watched the ambulance roll down the highway until it disappeared around a bend.

"What's going on here, Harry?" Rachel said. "How big a problem do you think we have?"

Harry pursed his lips and thought hard before answering. His emotions churned his stomach. "Too early to tell," he said finally. "But I think you should call a city council meeting. This town should be ready for anything."

17

Dante's Peak, way back, was a fur trading outpost in the Hudson's Bay Company days of the early 1800s. It grew from a settlement of a few hundred Indian trappers and white hunters to a small city in the middle 1880s when a short-lived gold and silver rush hit the area. Cold Creek, which ran through the town, became the Silver River, and a small boom drew a fresh and hopeful population from as far away as Boston.

Luckily, as the gold, silver, and lead mines petered out or leveled off in a matter of a few years, the long-simmering lumber business began to boom. In the late 1880s and '90s, the arrival of the railroads at Puget Sound brought cheap transportation. Lumbering took off and continued to be the mainstay of Dante's Peak and much of the Cascades until almost the present day. Until the great spotted owl controversy of the early 1990s.

Enforcement of the Endangered Species Act with regard to the northern spotted owl severely curtailed logging in the few remaining old-growth forests of all three West Coast states. Prosperous little towns like Dante's Peak all over the Cascades were scrambling to replace the economic lifeblood that logging had been for over a century.

The award from *Money* magazine all agreed, could go a long way toward helping Mayor Wando encourage others like Elliot Blair to bring their businesses and industries to this neighborly little town.

So long as there were no big surprises in store from the hulking snowcapped neighbor looking down on them from the north.

The city council chamber was a small boxy room in a very modest frame municipal hall. At the front of the chamber was a Washington State flag, a photograph of the governor, and a long, scarred worktable that served as dais. In the center of the room were several rows of badly worn vinyl chairs.

Including Rachel, there were seven on the council: Dr. Jane Fox; Mary Kelly, an insurance saleswoman; Norman Gates, a retired CPA; Karen Pope, an antique furniture dealer; Joe Ballard, the druggist; and William Collins, who was in dry goods. Also present were Sheriff Turner and, though he technically wasn't supposed to be, Les Worrell, the hardware store owner.

All these folks sat around the worktable, with Mayor Wando at the head.

Harry was in the hot seat. He sat alone at the other end.

"I thought this was supposed to be an *extinct* volcano," Sheriff Turner said.

"Not extinct, just dormant, as in sleeping," Harry said. "And your volcano might just be waking up."

"Mr. Dalton," Les Worrell said, "you are talking about the evacuation of seventy-four hundred people. Don't you think that's a little extreme?"

A loud murmur of agreement from almost all of those present.

"All I'm talking about," Harry said, "is that you consider alerting the town to the *possibility* of an evacuation."

Rachel nodded in agreement. "This way nobody will be caught off-guard should the situation suddenly deteriorate," she said.

"That's all very well and good," Les said. "But what Mr. Dalton doesn't realize is that if Elliot Blair gets the idea that there's some kind of problem around here, he is gonna take his eighteen million dollars and his eight hundred jobs and he is gonna evacuate." He paused, looked from face to face for emphasis, then said dramatically: "Then this town's gonna be dead and buried whether there's a volcano or not."

The council members all spoke at once, weighing in on both sides of the argument. Voices rose as indignation crept into the discourse on the sides of both the potential danger to life and limb and the possibly needless wasting of a much-needed economic infusion. Rachel tried to keep things orderly.

"Everybody, please—one at a time," she said. She

turned to Norman Gates. "Norman, pull out our emergency plans. I think we should at least take a look at them."

Norman got up and headed for the file cabinets. He riffled through some folders and came up with a thin file marked EMERGENCY/FOREST FIRE/MUDSLIDE/EARTHQUAKE. There wasn't even a heading for VOLCANO ERUPTION. The possibility had never seemed real. To most of the townspeople in the room, it still didn't.

18

An orange maxivan equipped with a satellite antenna drove into the peaceful town of Dante's Peak late in the afternoon. On the van's doors were the United States Department of the Interior Geological Survey logos: crossed fire axes on a white circular patch.

Paul Dreyfus and the full team from the Vancouver Observatory were on board: Terry Furlong, who'd built the robot Spider Legs, and the three young volcanologists, Nancy Field, Stan Tzima, and Greg Esmail.

They scoped the place out as they slowed to let the town veterinarian cross the street. He had an injured black bear cub in his arms and was talking to it soothingly. Townsfolk smiled and said endearing things to the cub as they passed, as though the vet had his infant out for a walk.

"Look at this nice little town," Stan said, "nestled all snug and cozy against the mountain."

"Yeah," Nancy said, scoffing. "Just like Pompeii."

They all smiled a little sardonically. They had seen too many towns like this—unsuspecting, unafraid, trusting that the reassuringly calm past was indication of a similarly uneventful future. Carrying images of numerous catastrophic before-and-afters in their minds made these professional field scientists a bit hardened, prone to graveyard humor.

"I hope nobody just remodeled their kitchen," Greg said. They all groaned at the cruel thought. Greg was adept at the black-humor end of the job, having already been a touch hardened by life when he came to volcanology.

Born in Pakistan, he was the youngest, most energetic and rebellious son of a large family headed by a wealthy ophthalmologist. He was at university grudgingly studying to be an eye doctor when events conspired to set him on a zigzag path to becoming the team's youngest volcanologist.

There was in Karachi at that time, and still is, a criminal practice that seems strange to Westerners—house invasion robberies carried out by gangs of thugs who call a house in an affluent neighborhood and warn the occupants they are coming. "Please have goods, money, and jewelry ready," they'll say. Calling the corrupt, on-the-take police for help is an exercise in futility. So homeowners, if they lack their own private security force, simply cave to the robbers' demands and cut their losses.

Often the robbers require the family to feed them a

nice meal while they are there collecting the loot. This was the situation one evening at Greg's parents' house when he walked in. He went insane—managed to maim two of the surprised robbers with a fireplace poker, and a third almost died.

This isn't the way things are done in Karachi.

A representative of the other gangs and a police lieutenant came to the house and offered a deal: Greg would leave the country and ward off bloody, politically embarrassing reprisals. In return his sizable extended family would be declared off-limits and their fortune and lives would be safe.

Within two weeks, Greg was in Miami living with a cousin, enrolled in the MBA program at the University of Miami.

He lasted a semester and a half as an MBA candidate.

He met a female geology student who took him with her on spring break to the Soufriére Hills on the Caribbean Island of Montserrat, where the volcano was rumbling and venting and showing other signs of acting up. Greg was thrilled. Volcano fieldwork: What better vocation for a young claustrophobic guy full of energy? He transferred to the physical sciences the day he got back.

Now, as he arrived with the USGS team at this increasingly promising site, he was excited. He, like the Harry of earlier days, embodied the central contradiction of all geologists, who were immersed, perforce, in geologic time: He was dying to see something *move*.

Paul pulled the van into the gravel parking lot at Cluster's Motel. The group got out and stretched, looking around for Harry's customized orange Suburban.

Dreyfus went inside to register and find a place to put their operation on the ground.

Warren Cluster took a mind-one's-own-business attitude toward his motel guests. He didn't know what these seismology nerds were doing up here and he wouldn't give a chicken's gizzard to find out. He was looking to the future, picturing the day when his optimally located, soon-to-be-expanded motel would be overflowing with free-spending skiers and resort-goers.

"The conference room oughta be big enough for you to set up shop in," he grumbled to Dreyfus. He'd charge 'em double the rate of a usual room, he was thinking. Government money, after all.

"Thanks," Dreyfus said, handing over his government-issue credit card. "Would you happen to know where I can find Harry Dalton? I thought he'd be here."

"He's over at the city council chambers," Cluster said. "He and the mayor called a meeting."

Dreyfus's features darkened. This was exactly what he was afraid of.

19

In the city council chambers, the lively discussion was still under way as Rachel looked over the town's evacuation plan.

"So when is this mountain likely to blow up?" Norman said. He was a CPA by training; he wanted facts and figures.

"I wish that predicting volcanic eruptions was an exact science," Harry began, "but unfortunately—"

Les saw his future fading away. He shouted: "Perfect! So we put the town on notice and nothing happens." He stood up and waved his arms. "People," he said, "it's not like we're the only town in the Cascades with a great ski mountain. We can't risk losing Blair Industries on account of Mr. Dalton's wild guesses!"

Dr. Fox tried to lower the temperature by speaking

quietly. "What we can't risk losing," she said, "are the lives of our citizens because you happen to be in escrow with them on a piece of *your* land."

"It's not about my land, Jane," Les said heatedly.

Rachel looked up from the evacuation plan. It was time to bring the meeting to a head, she saw. "Okay, everybody," she said. "Let's put it to a vote. Do we or do we not put Dante's Peak on an evacuation alert?"

The door at the back of the chambers swung open, and everyone turned to look.

Harry was startled. "Paul!" he said.

Everybody watched as Dreyfus walked in and approached the front of the room. He moved with a confident air of authority, not shy about walking in uninvited.

"Everybody, this is my boss," Harry said, "Dr. Paul Dreyfus."

Dreyfus had a warm smile for everybody but Harry. "A pleasure," he said. Turning to Harry, he asked, "What's going on here?"

"I've recommended to the council members that they put this town on alert," Harry said. "They were just about to vote on it."

"Harry, can I have a word with you?" Dreyfus said.

Harry walked over and joined Dreyfus and they stepped out into the corridor.

"Look, Harry," Dreyfus said, "I sent you up here to take a look around, not to scare the hell out of the city council."

Harry was stunned. "I know, Paul," he said, "but there are two people dead. Recommending an alert seemed the only responsible thing to do."

Dreyfus shook his head. "You know, there are dozens of explanations to account for what happened at those hot springs," he said. "Anything from a mild earthquake to a slight seismic shift to subsidence to underground erosion to—"

"Paul—" Harry interrupted.

"—And not one of those reasons," Dreyfus said, "not one of them, means that this mountain is going to erupt next week, next month, or in the next hundred years."

Dreyfus stared Harry down.

Then turned on his heel and went back into the room to address the council members. Harry followed him in and stood at the back of the room.

"Ladies and gentlemen," Dreyfus said, walking to the head of the table, "I'm sure Dr. Dalton was doing what he thought was in the best interests of your town. However, I have learned from bitter experience that these decisions are not to be made lightly."

Les and the other businessmen perked up and listened with mounting interest.

Dreyfus smiled reassuringly. "Back in 1980," he said, "I'd have bet you a million bucks that Mammoth Mountain was gonna go up. A tremendous amount of geologic activity, nearly continuous swarms of earthquakes, a dome of hot magma rising, trees dying from carbon dioxide gas seepage—all the signs." He shrugged. "We began talking about putting the town on alert. Well, thank God, Mammoth didn't go up, but the damage had already been done. Word had gotten out that the United States Geological Survey had 'expressed some concern'—just that; no more—and the tourists panicked and stayed away. The town nearly went bankrupt. So now I'm a lot more cautious when it comes to even *talking* about putting a town on alert."

Dreyfus was impressive and persuasive. Harry could see that this was exactly what most of the town burghers wanted to hear.

"Folks," Dreyfus said, "we're gonna be camped out here for as long as it takes with seismometers and tilt meters that will measure and monitor every hiccup your mountain makes; we're gonna be bouncing laser beams off it to track changes in size, analyzing gas emissions . . . Hell, we've even got a robot that's gonna take a stroll up there and take the darned thing's temperature. The point that I'm making is—if there is any call for an alert, it'll be based on scientific evidence. *Not* on anyone's opinion."

He was done. The council members all looked at each other—and ganged up on Rachel.

"For God sakes, Rachel," Mary Kelly, the insurance agent, said, "this thing should have been handled much more discreetly. This meeting should never have been called."

Les wagged a finger at her. "I just hope our Mr. Blair hasn't got wind of this," he said. "If he has, salvaging the deal will call for some serious damage control."

Norman Gates was more direct. "If Blair Industries gets scared off," he said to Rachel, "we're holding you responsible . . . *Mayor*."

Rachel didn't know what to think. This man Harry had seemed just as levelheaded and responsible as Dreyfus.

Was he that far off base? She glared across at him, trying to decide.

Dreyfus walked over to Harry and locked eyes with him. Harry was completely unrepentant. "You're making a big mistake here, Paul," he said flatly. "This is an unstable system and this town should be on alert." He wanted to add that it was only fair to be on the safe side in a remote place like this where evacuation, if it came to that, would be slow, difficult, and hazardous. But the I've-had-it-with-you expression on Paul's face stopped him.

"You wanted to go on vacation, didn't you, Harry?" Dreyfus said. "See you in two weeks."

Harry, humiliated, stormed out of the room.

Rachel watched him go, confused about the whole thing.

The rest of the council, reassured, was now chuckling and chattering in relief among themselves.

Rachel still felt a disquiet as she packed the disaster evacuation file away. She walked out of the room alone, a pariah, at least for now.

20

At Crater Lake, as the sun was getting big and orange in the western sky, a shudder in the ground loosed a section of bank and it fell away into the water.

The mini-landslide left behind the exposed, cutaway burrow of a muskrat family. The mama muskrat was crouched in the central chamber, fat and healthy-looking from a season of good foraging; but unmoving. Lying next to her, also healthy-looking and also unmoving, were half a dozen furry babies. All were dead. Asphyxiated. They, like the rest of the burrowing animals in this area and other areas on the flanks of Dante's Peak, didn't have a chance. A silent killer had crept in and taken them in their sleep.

Pine needles fell from a tree above. Brown and dead, they drifted in the breeze. Several acres of trees above the lake were dying.

Harry strode out of the council chambers in a black, black mood. He was being wrongly pilloried. He resented it. And he had a sick feeling that he was failing at the thing at which he most wanted and needed to succeed.

Harry threw himself in his Suburban and wheeled it around in the direction of Cluster's Motel.

He drove through the town, where life was going on as usual. Graham Wando, coasting his bike toward the Blue Moon Cafe, gave a wave. Harry didn't see him, just sped on, eyes ahead, jaw set.

At the motel he passed the USGS vehicle parked in the lot without stopping to greet his colleagues. He went straight to his room and started to get his things together. He wanted to get the hell out of there ASAP.

But while he was throwing his things into his big duffel bag, he glanced out the window. He saw something—a little drama unfolding in the parking lot. He tried to ignore it, but couldn't help himself. He stopped what he was doing and drifted to the window and watched.

It was Cluster, the ornery, stiff-backed owner, having a heated conversation with a good-looking younger woman with red lips, big hair, and high-heeled white boots. She seemed a little unsteady on her feet as she argued and stuck her finger in Cluster's face. She flounced into her pickup and smiled at the seven-year-old boy in the passenger seat as she keyed the ignition. She jammed the truck in gear—but went only a foot or two. Cluster stood square in front of the pickup and wouldn't move.

The woman swore at him. Cluster just stood his ground and shook his head no. The woman sat there for a moment contemplating vehicular homicide. Then she reached over, kissed the little boy, and shooed him out of the truck. The boy ran to Cluster, and the woman goosed the accelerator and squealed away. Cluster, the sourpussed old hickory stick, swept the giggling boy up in his arms and walked off toward the office, his smile radiating love like a supernova.

Harry stood there for another minute gazing out at the quiet parking lot. A look of resolve slowly formed on his face. He took his clothes and put them back in the closet.

21

Stein's Bar was the best Dante's Peak had to offer in the way of sports/pool bars with a little decent music. Two medium-sized, four-quarters-in-the-slot pool tables with worn but intact felt. One large-screen TV over the bar. A full complement of Washington State microbrewery beers as well as assorted national and Canadian brands. And at the back, a small stage where drums and keyboards were set up and a chalkboard announced ORANGE INSANITY BLUES BAND, coming Thursday.

Paul Dreyfus and the volcano SWAT team were walking through town after dinner when they spotted Stein's.

"Shall we?" Dreyfus said.

"Looks authentic," Nancy said. She was the first one through the door.

They all stood inside the door letting their eyes adjust to the smoky dimness and listening to two dudes at the nearest pool table playing and jawing.

"Did you get work?" the first dude asked.

"Nah," said the second. He shot and scratched. "I shoulda gone home a long time ago, but I been rotating around havin' some fun."

Dreyfus looked close at the one other customer there, hunched at the bar sucking on a long-neck ale. It was Harry.

The others saw him and looked at each other in surprise. Dreyfus motioned them off toward a table in the back. He went over to the bar and took the stool next to Harry.

"I thought you'd be off on your fishing trip by now," Dreyfus said.

"I decided to stick around," Harry said.

"I can see that," Dreyfus said. "Why?"

"Because this town's in trouble and I'm the best man you've got."

Dreyfus didn't say anything. Then: "You are the best man I've got." He thought about that while signaling to the bartender for a draft. Then he turned on his stool and faced Harry. "But unless you can get it through your head that there are politics involved in a situation like this, delicate politics, not to mention economics," he said, "then you're only going to do these people harm, not good."

Harry nodded and said with sincerity, "I understand."

Dreyfus watched him closely. And made a decision. "Tomorrow morning I want to hire a chopper," he said.

"Fly around the mountain and take some COSPEC readings. I want to see if there's any sulfur dioxide up there."

Harry nodded. He was back on board. He and Dreyfus were in accord. For now. "Done," Harry said.

"And remember," Dreyfus said, "from now on everything comes from me. If there are any more town meetings to be called, I'll be the one to call them. Okay?"

"Okay, Paul," Harry said.

Dreyfus motioned with his head. They both picked up their beers and walked over to join the rest of the team at the table.

Harry had great respect for Paul Dreyfus, and also some reservations. Paul catered too much to political interests for Harry's taste. He was forever hedging his bets and trimming the institute's sails—and those of his team—to fit prevailing winds at regional head-quarters and in Washington, D.C. He had the habit of soliciting advice and opinions ad nauseam, Harry felt, before he would ever pull the trigger. It drove Harry nuts.

Of course, that was why Dreyfus had risen to his position of prominence in the USGS—his political acumen; along with the fact that he was a first-rate geophysicist.

Harry knew it hadn't all been handed to Paul, that he'd had to struggle for what he had. And the fact that part of his struggle had been against his own twisted nature made Dreyfus a sympathetic figure to his colleagues.

Paul was a problem child, no other way to put it. Growing up in the town of East Aurora in upstate New York, he was a disastrous student right from the first. Not reading in the second grade, couldn't tell time until the fourth, nearly flunked sixth. But it was his attitude toward the laws of society and of gravity—an impetuous disinclination to think things through—that kept him in constant hot water.

He liked pelting school windows and metal road signs with rocks, for the glorious sounds it made. He broke both arms riding his bicycle along the top of a stone wall on a dare. He shattered his older brother's collarbone by jumping on him off the garage to surprise him. When he got a real bow and a dozen feathered target arrows for his birthday, he lay on his back with his feet up holding the bow and shot all of the arrows as far as he could up the side of the mountain behind their house. He never found a one of them.

"Judgment, Paul! Judgment," his father said over and over again in exasperation.

In high school Dreyfus showed great aptitude in science and mathematics, but was more interested in supercharging motorbikes and old golf carts and racing them on dirt ovals than in schoolwork. Anything that involved trying something new that he could accomplish with direct action Paul liked. He played hooky from his whole second semester at college to help a friend achieve his dream of building a communal tree house in Vermont.

His father, the head of the Applied Math Department at the University of Buffalo, was beyond furious. To make it up to him for wasting all that tuition, Paul impulsively planned a big surprise party for his father, inviting a roster of his important friends and colleagues from the university. He prepared everything himself, and on the evening in question, got dressed up and announced to his parents what was in store. His father thought about it for a minute, then said, "I'm sorry, Paul. We have other plans." He and Paul's mother went out and left Paul to fend for himself: receive the guests, explain as best he could, and conduct a dinner party in the absence of the guest of honor.

Paul was humiliated. And changed forever, as his father had hoped. He went back to college and applied himself. He vowed never to do things on impulse again, to avoid impetuous decisions at all costs. He took counsel from friends and mentors before all big choices, and sometimes seemed to have an aversion to committing himself to action.

It was that modus operandi Dreyfus brought to his job at the USGS. He always thought long and hard and sought the counsel of others—many others—before loosing the arrow.

The one exception had been Mammoth Mountain. There he had given in to instinct and impulse, and called a premature alert. It had brought back all the shame and mortification of his youth.

Never again, he'd vowed.

22

The Blue Moon Cafe was the best place in town for breakfast and lunch. People came for the good food. But fine as it was, the food was secondary to the coffees, which were great, and the context. The Blue Moon Cafe was the "third place" in town, after home and work. It was the place to connect, to wire in to the nervous system of the area. It was the Internet of Dante's Peak and several other small towns nearby.

Some customers swore that the coffee craze that was sweeping the Northwest—gourmet coffee bars on every corner in every city and town—actually started with Rachel at the Blue Moon Cafe. They said she was the first to serve Jamaica Blue Mountain outside of Jamaica. The tendency toward tall tales in the Pacific Northwest notwithstanding, Rachel's coffee was supernal and was certainly one of the catalysts for the vivid sense of community that prevailed in her cafe.

Rachel, at the cash register, was taking payment for breakfast from Michael and Jessica—and accepting major hugs from each. The young couple walked out happy; they now had enough money for the down payment on their first house. Rachel had just quietly arranged a personal loan for them from the town soft touch, Matthew Hale, a retired options arbitrageur who was the cafe's first customer every morning.

Rachel took fresh-ground specialty coffees to a table where Pete Prugo the plumber sat with Tony the barber and Dick Boyd the car paint distributor. Dick had brought in a pound of a new Sulawesi varietal he'd gotten from a client—a gift for Rachel.

Dick Boyd, a compact man with a bushy mustache, a Billy-Goat-Gruff voice, and a twinkly smile, was one of those rare people who had the system figured out. He ran his business; kept up a nice house, had four cars, two kids in parochial school, and a contented wife, and went on family vacations twice a year. And he still had the time and money to do all the things he liked: fish, go skiing, play with his computers, and sit in sports bars telling lies with his cronies. He was the idol of many a struggling younger man in town.

A chunky white-bearded man at a table by the door raised a meek finger to Rachel. She went over and refilled his coffee cup and gave him a pat on the back. The man—she knew him as Chief Vincent—nodded his thanks. "One has to be on the corner when the bus comes by," he said. He bent again to his work—writing like mad in a lined ledger.

The Chief was a fixture at that table when he was in town. Rachel gave him a free breakfast or lunch when he was low on cash, which was almost always.

Over this last year Rachel had pieced together his story. Vincent Chieffo had been a powerhouse litigation attorney in New York until, on a summer visit to Martha's Vineyard, he had gone out alone in a canoe on a pond and had some sort of epiphany. A flash of light, he remembered, and an overwhelming moment of peace during which he heard the voices of man and nature intermingling. And he was changed. He resigned the practice of law, took a leave from his family, and moved back to Washington State, where he'd been born.

Now, as "Chief Vincent," he spent his mornings and nights writing *The Oral History of Bars*—"Section One: The Cascades" in his ledger books. He whiled away the afternoons drifting in his canoe on one or another of the many lakes of the Cascades, awaiting another flash of light, it was said.

Rachel cleared his breakfast dishes and was piling them on the busing cart when Harry walked in. Rachel was surprised to see him.

"Good morning," Harry said.

Rachel nodded politely, but it was clear she was still a bit angry about the town council meeting. Harry took a seat at the counter.

"Coffee?" Rachel said.

"Please," Harry said.

"Espresso, cappuccino, cafe latte," she said. "What would you like?"

"Have you got any regular coffee?" he said.

Rachel picked up a coffeepot. "I thought you left town last night."

"I decided to stay," he said. "See what new trouble I can get myself into."

Rachel almost smiled. Harry moved his cup over, and Rachel poured.

"So," he said, "what's good here?"

"Everything's good here," she said, looking up at him.

"Oww!" Harry said, pulling his hand back.

Rachel had accidentally spilled some coffee on him. "Oh, I'm sorry," she said.

Harry managed a rueful half smile. "I suppose I had that coming for screwing up your reelection chances."

Rachel gave a genuine smile. "I didn't do it on purpose," she said.

"Neither did I," Harry said.

Rachel tilted her head and contemplated him a moment, then nodded. "I know," she said.

"I've always been better at figuring out volcanoes than at figuring out people and politics," Harry said. "Anyway, I really am sorry if I caused you any trouble. I only wanted to help."

Rachel put the coffeepot back on the warmer and just looked at him. Then she made up her mind. "Do you like eggplant lasagna?"

Harry laughed. "For breakfast?"

"For dinner. I'm inviting you for dinner," she said. "As a way of saying thank you."

"Thanks for what?" he said, surprised.

"For saving my son's life yesterday," she said. "And for caring about us."

Harry smiled his appreciation.

23

Harry and Terry Furlong would be the first up the mountain for a close look.

Terry was as different from Harry as night and day. The stocky volcanologist in the loud shirts had come to the volatile science by way of the more staid discipline of mechanical engineering. He was building robots for NASA at Carnegie-Mellon University in Pittsburgh when the USGS came calling. The USGS had a more earthbound need for terrain crawlers than NASA, but the obstacles were just the same. Go in where no man could safely go and bring back the goods.

Terry, in his early thirties and unmarried, was the happiest guy around. He was a mechanical wunderkind who had his dream job: Erector sets for pay; transformers at life size. And he still had a kid's sense of humor. He specialized in practical jokes and booby traps that had his colleagues always watching where they put their feet.

He had been known to put blacking on the eyepiece of binoculars, to load up the towels in the bathroom with shaving cream, to rig up a compatriot's desk chair so it would slowly descend to the floor when he or she sat down, and to rig up their computers so that the machines would laugh hysterically at the first entry.

Nancy and Greg got back at him by lining his baseball cap with atomic balm and rigging his personal fan with baby powder.

Terry's contribution to the team was preventing too high a level of maturity from setting in; in reality, preventing them from letting the frequent grimness and danger of their jobs get them down.

The Bell 204 helicopter with Harry and Terry aboard took off from its home base next to the Trout Springs Ranger Station at the intersection of Rural Route 23 and County Route 12. It was an aging green and orange number that hired out for logging and firefighting.

The contract pilot—"R. Hutcherson," according to the tag on his bomber jacket—was mute and anonymous behind his Assassin aviator shades as he lifted the ship at a conservative angle and swung over the ranger station at low revs. Hutcherson got a lot of assignments from the Forestry Service rangers and took care not to jeopardize the relationship with any hotdogging in their vicinity.

Once he'd got the copter around the brow of the first

hill and out of sight lines from the station, however, he jacked the revs, turned the ship on its side, and did an incredibly high-Gs, high-stress swerve up a narrow canyon. He headed the ship toward the steeper slopes of Dante's Peak, rolling side to side as they went streaking up winding ravines and canyons.

Harry and Terry just stared at each other and went to work tightening their shoulder harnesses. When they again looked up, the copter was headed straight at a granite cliff face as inpossibly high and impassable as Yosemite's Half Dome. Hutcherson cranked the stick back and sent the tiny machine roaring straight up the face of the cliff and over the top like it was a thrill ride.

"Where'd you learn to fly like that?" Harry said, once they had leveled out.

"Veet-nam," Hutcherson said. "Hmong Hills. Same dealy as here—one wrong twitch and you're imbedded." He laughed raucously. Then was racked with a brief coughing nic fit. Then calmed down.

"I should warn you," Harry said, "when we get to the volcano—"

"I know, don't worry, all business," Hutcherson said. "Hot updrafts, microbursts, ash in the carbs, toxic gases—I've flown volcanoes. I was all over Mount St. Helens. Except the day she blew. I had the flu. Or I'd be dead." He laughed again, but stopped quickly as he remembered the awesome power displayed that day.

Harry decided to say no more. He'd rather have a slightly hotdoggy *good* pilot than an unimaginative tyro, in case of trouble.

The helicopter banked around the side of Dante's Peak near the summit.

A COSPEC inside the chopper took gas readings. A COSPEC was a spectrometer that analyzed the light above fissures and crevasses, looking for the signature wavelengths of carbon dioxide, sulfur dioxide, and other telltale volcanic gases. Harry and Terry monitored the readings.

Harry gave pilot Hutcherson some new directions. "Okay, let's cover that rift there," he said, pointing. "As low as you can get and right up through into the caldera."

Now the shoe was on the other foot. Harry was asking for crater flying, which made the pilot's testicles contract and his stomach queasy. He'd never admit it, though. "If I work through my lunch hour," he said, irritated, "it's overtime."

Terry growled, "Just do it."

R. Hutcherson was cowed. The chopper banked and arrowed down in the deep gorge.

Harry and Terry watched their instruments, glancing up every few seconds. Hutcherson kept his eyes far up the rift, anticipating the demands of flying in tight quarters over possible superheated gas vents. None of the three saw what happened right in front of and below the chopper as it flew over.

One moment a formation of rock stood as it had for ages, immovable, immutable. The next instant the terrain trembled and the rock began to split. The formation fell away like water, leaving behind a raw, bleached wound in the crag. The men roaring past in the helicopter just above could not hope to see or hear it.

Terry and Harry were scanning their gas readings.

"Well, you're the man with the instincts," Terry said.

"Some sulfur dioxide emissions," Harry said, "but not enough to worry about." He looked across the crater as the copter crested the rift and started to loop away. "Looks okay."

Hutcherson waited a couple of beats for further directions. Hearing none, he breathed an inward sigh of relief and put the machine into a steep dive. They screamed down a sheer wall and swooped out into a broad valley, heading away from the devil's mouth.

24

Rachel's home was not Martha Stewart country. Mismatched furniture competed with kids' toys, and school and sports clutter for valuable space in the modest three-bedroom house.

In the living room, Native American Cochina dolls stood atop the pioneer-era hutch cupboard filled with Lauren's collections of plastic horses, stuffies, and beanbag animals. Across from the hutch cupboard reared an elegant nineteenth century English highboy reproduction, next to a secondhand Eames chair. Both these Rachel had bought from Karen Pope to help her get her shop started three years before, promising not to put them next to each other.

Dinner was over. Rachel was making coffee. Harry was showing Graham and Lauren a falling-dominoes trick at the table. Harry waved an imaginary wand over the black pieces and started the toppling seemingly without touching them. The kids were suspicious, smiling. Rachel, watching from across the room, smiled at the kids' reaction.

"I brought you something," Harry said, and pulled out a package. "A game that was found in ancient Egyptian temples from five thousand years ago . . ." The kids' eyes bugged.

Crickets sang quietly all around them as Rachel and Harry had coffee outside on her porch.

The kids were inside trying to play the game Harry had brought—a game called Mancala that was actually new to them. So far they had not cracked the wooden game board, lost or eaten any of the glass counters, or killed each other.

"I know it's just a little town," Rachel said to Harry as they sat in the dark, "but I can't imagine living anyplace else. I grew up here. Went to school here."

"Got married here?" Harry said.

Rachel nodded sadly.

Harry gave her the space to talk about it or not. He drank from his mug of coffee and listened to the crickets.

"Brian and I were just kids when we got married," she said. "We haven't heard from him in a little while." She gave a sad laugh. "'A little while'—try six years."

More crickets.

"You'd never get her to admit it," Rachel said, "but I doubt if Ruth even knows where he is."

"You seem like you're doing okay," Harry said.

"It took a while, but yeah," Rachel said. "The kids and me, we *are* doing okay."

Rachel felt at ease with this man. She realized she had the urge—which she resisted—to pour out the story to him of her ill-starred marriage. How just at the point her young life seemed to be coming properly together, it was actually about to crash down.

Rachel had graduated from Hood College in Oregon, full of energy and a desire to do everything all at once. She'd been a government major, and she went to Washington, D.C., to work in the office of her congressman, imbued with the desire to serve. Her job was legislative researcher. She spent her days cooped up in her office, in the library, on the phone, costing out the constant stream of proposals the lumbering and mining interests sent to their congressman for his backing.

She was going crazy.

Most of the men who pursued her—in a town where the ratio of single women to single men was three to one—were married. The unattached men she met tended to be hyperambitious workaholics looking for a home secretary they could also have sex with.

Her roommate got mugged. That did it.

Rachel helped her pack her bags; then, on impulse, packed her own and went off with her to join what they called the Foreign Legion. That is, they signed on with TWA to be flight attendants and set out to see the world.

It was Rachel's season in the sun. Her wild streak came out. She stayed in every fancy hotel from Djibouti to Jakarta, partied in every cool and funky bar and club in all the world's capitals. She had wine and fun, and more romance than any one girl could respectably admit to.

She was tiring of it, and had just arranged to be based in Seattle in order to be closer to her hometown in the mountains, when she met Brian. Brian was a cabinetmaker from a town in the same part of the Cascades, in Seattle trying to get a handmade-furniture export business going.

They fell for each other as hard and absolutely as two people ever did. It was simply *right*. They moved in together after four weeks, and got married three months later. Graham came along quite quickly, and Rachel prevailed upon Brian to move back to the mountains.

He was in love, he was a responsible young guy, so he sucked it up and did it. He set up his woodworking shop in Dante's Peak, conceived a daughter, brought home the bacon, and loved his family.

But it all had a cost. The truth was Brian hated small towns. When he married Rachel he thought he was marrying a city girl, a soul mate who would go out and challenge the wide world with him. Instead, he gave up his big dreams and moved back to purgatory. It couldn't last. It didn't.

"What about you?" Rachel asked Harry. "Ever been married?"

"No," he said. "Never . . ."

"How come?

"Well, for one thing," he said, "I move around a lot—Colombia, Guatemala, the Philippines, Mexico, New Guinea, New Zealand; wherever there's a volcano with an attitude problem. It makes it tough to settle down."

"Ever been close?"

Harry didn't answer right away. The pain showed on his face. "Yes," he said. "Once.

"Touchy subject?" Rachel said.

"Her name was Marianne," he said. "We worked together. She loved volcanoes—they fascinated her. She loved the life, maybe even more than I did. Five years ago, a volcano called Galeras erupted in Colombia. Marianne and I, we thought we had enough time to get out, but unfortunately we were wrong. . . . We stayed too long to watch the show. Marianne was killed."

"I'm sorry," Rachel.

"It's crazy to take chances with volcanoes," Harry said. "There are too many ways to *lose*." He was staring up at the mountain. "If she does a Mount St. Helens, the blast would get here within a minute."

"I hope you're wrong about our volcano, Harry," she said. "But if you're not, well . . . I'm glad you're here."

Harry smiled.

25

Cluster's Motel had no restaurant. Cluster kept a box of stale donuts and a pot of black coffee brewing at the front desk for motel guests, but the coffee was as sour as he often was.

Rachel's Land Cruiser pulled into the parking lot. She got out, carrying a boxful of coffees in "to-go" cups. Cluster's coffee was not her idea of hospitality.

The pine-paneled motel conference room had been converted into a temporary observatory—the USGS war room.

One video monitor was devoted entirely to weather satellite information. Another scrolled infrared satellite images of thermal activity.

Taped to the walls next to the mountain landscape painting were detailed topographic terrain maps of the area. A variety of sensing instruments had been set up on tables or were still in their special foam-lined metal cases.

The whole team was there, doing the unpacking, already at work on their big, powerful laptops. Harry and Terry, getting ready to head off, were talking to Stan.

"We brought along five seismometers," Stan said. "Think that'll do it?"

"I'd say so," Harry said.

Just then Rachel walked in with the box of hot coffees. She and Harry were obviously glad to see each other.

"Good morning," he said.

"Good morning, Harry," she said. "I thought you guys might like some coffee. I don't know what kind of coffee you like. I just did cappuccino all around. And yours was regular, right?"

Terry noticed the look that passed between Harry and Rachel as she handed him his coffee. He smiled and gave Harry a playful nudge. Harry glared at him and tried to look completely innocent at the same time.

Greg, smelling the coffee aroma from across the room, homed in on Rachel like a magnet. "I'm jonesing, man," he said, his eyes taking on a seraphic gleam like an opium addict smelling the pipe. "I need a good fix," he said with a grin. "What kind of coffee machine d'you use?"

"Gaggia," Rachel said.

Greg nodded. Like a wine taster, he took a sip of his coffee. "Where do you get your beans?" he said casually.

"Doctor Espresso in Berkeley," Rachel said, waiting

for the verdict. There was nobody tougher than a true coffee connoisseur.

"You keep the beans in the freezer?" Greg said, again casually.

"Never," Rachel said. "Never put coffee in the freezer. The beans lose all their oils."

It was a test, she knew. And she passed. Greg smiled and turned to Harry.

"This town might just be worth saving after all," he said.

26

Harry, Terry, Stan, and Nancy were all up on the mountain working on one of the ten areas of Dante's Peak that their game plan designated for wiring, miking, taping, or electronically smelling.

This spot was a flank of the mountain about halfway to the summit, on a northeast-facing slope, with no sight lines whatsoever—hence no clear radio telemetry lines—to USGS field headquarters down at Cluster's Motel. They didn't need it. For transmitting data they had a satellite transponder set up on a rocky promontory, hooked to the tilt meter, strain gauge, and seismic amplifier.

Terry watched as Harry placed a seismometer, a device that measured earth disturbances—earthquakes, nuclear blasts, and in this case volcanic tremors—into the shallow hole he had dug. The seismometer looked like a softball-sized jug with a cable coming out the top. He packed dirt tightly around the device and covered it completely, tamping it down so it wouldn't move. He ran the cable along the ground to the amplifier and on to the transponder.

"Nice woman, Rachel," Terry said as they worked. "Best-looking mayor I've ever seen."

"That ought to do it," Harry said, ignoring Terry's fishing line. He checked the connections and turned the power on. "Go take a look."

Terry climbed up to where Stan was perched atop a rock outcropping, wiring in the ruggedized laptop computer. Harry waited until Stan got a steady signal from the instruments. Stan pointed to him. Harry stomped his foot on the ground. On the computer screen, where a horizontal seismic line was crawling across evenly, a small spike appeared, a reaction to Harry's foot hitting the ground.

"Perfecto!" Stan called. "If this mountain really is quaking, we're gonna know about it."

Stan Tzima never seemed to tire of the drudgery involved in his job—the lugging, assembling, digging, monitoring, hiking. He never tired and he never complained. It was a trait that came out of his background.

Stan Tzima grew up in a traditional Chinese-American family in the Bay area. He was the middle child in a family of nine kids. Stan, like every one of his siblings, was a standout student. He excelled in all subjects through his junior year in high school. Then, inexplicably, he became a gangster, San Francisco

Chinatown style. He smoked and ran dope and swore allegiance to the Black Hand, a junior Tong group.

When he was arrested and charged—and given probation—the only explanation he could come up with for his father was that he was committed to becoming something other than himself.

Fine, his father said. You're a steelworker.

Stan's penance was an enforced two-year stint at the Fontana Steel Mills in southern California, in the years before U.S. steel production got beat into the ground by overseas production.

He was put to work as an ingot wrangler, doing heavy labor around the open hearths. It was brutal work—incredibly hot, demanding, dangerous. And he quickly realized it lacked the intellectual content he would have to have in his day-to-day job.

But he did get something out of it besides a good lesson in the hard realities of real life: He found that the behavior of molten iron and carbon and other materials intrigued him.

He started reading metallurgy on his own. And when he left his two-year purgatory at Fontana he enrolled in the Colorado School of Mines. He discovered that the commercial uses of ores and metals didn't interest him that much, but that the natural provenances and evolutions of them did.

It was a short jump from there to wanting to watch minerals come out of the deep earth in their primeval state; from mining engineering to volcanology.

His father was the first to embrace him when he came down off the stand with his doctorate in geophysics. And his father insisted, when Paul Dreyfus offered him a job, that the young man come clean to Dreyfus about his checkered past. Dreyfus smiled indulgently and welcomed the sinner aboard.

Harry and the others began packing up the instrument cases to lug them back down to the van. The mountain was now bugged.

Along with other seismometers, they had installed tilt meters to measure even the slightest change in the angle of the ground and laser receptors to monitor any changes in the mountain's size. And this was just the outside of the beast. They had yet to look in its mouth and stick any of their instruments in there.

The movement of magma in the enormous cavities in the belly of the beast was what they were setting up to track. Swarms of quakes originating in different parts of the earth under the mountain, deformation of the caldera's surface—these things meant magma near the surface, on the move; meant an eruption could be imminent.

The year before, on Mount Akautan in Alaska, their instruments had measured seventeen hundred small earthquakes on just the third day they were there. Two-thousand-degree molten magma on the move in a big way. They'd upgraded that smoker in the Aleutian Islands to Code Orange, a Level B notice, second highest, meaning it could blow at any time. And they'd got back to a safe distance, fast.

As Terry helped Harry put away a backpack, he tried a more direct tack. "So how was dinner last night?" he said.

Harry kept working. "Do me a favor, Terry," he said. "Don't try to fix me up."

"I have great taste in women," he said. "When have I ever steered you wrong?"

"What about Astrid?" Harry said.

"I thought you'd have lots in common," Terry said. "She said she was into rocks."

"Crystals, Terry," Harry said. "Crystals. Not rocks." Terry shrugged. Who knew?

27

Harry, Nancy, and Stan were gathered in the Cluster's Motel parking lot watching Terry put Spider Legs through his premission paces.

Rachel's Land Cruiser pulled in.

She waved, parked. She lifted her tray of coffees out of the back. The team had been there only three days but already she knew everybody's preference. She moved from person to person, dispensing hospitality: "Decaf espresso . . . double cappuccino . . . filter no milk . . . double-percent latte . . . single espresso . . ." She looked around for Greg and Dreyfus.

Inside the temporary observatory, Dreyfus and Greg were manning the video monitors, watching the pictures Spider Legs was sending from right outside. Greg leapt up excitedly when Rachel appeared on one of the monitors.

"It's coffee time!" he said. He rushed out. Dreyfus remained behind, shaking his head.

Rachel saw Greg charging out the door. She bestowed his custom-designed filter-no-milk, Costa Rica Tres Rios Double-Dark Roast on the eager cafophile. He lifted the lid and stole a whiff, then rushed back inside to drink it.

Rachel put on her citizen-mayor hat and got the latest from Nancy as she savored her coffee. "So, how's it looking?" she asked.

"We've been recording between twenty-five to seventy-five earthquakes per day," Nancy said matter-of-factly.

Rachel panicked. "Oh, my God!" she said, almost dropping the coffee tray. Harry laughed and steadied her.

"Don't worry. They're microquakes," Stan said. "They happen all the time."

Rachel gave him a look: Huh? "Oh, well, thank God for that," she said. She checked out Spider Legs. "What's this thing for?" she said to Harry.

"Spider Legs," Harry said, "is designed to go where it's too dangerous for us."

"It's going to gather and analyze high-temperature gases from fumaroles," Terry said, "and send pictures back here to home base."

"Spider Legs," Rachel said thoughtfully. *Fumaroles?*

The robot, going through its paces, abruptly stopped and turned toward her as though he had heard her speak his name. Rachel's eyes widened. At the controls, Terry grinned.

Inside, Greg operated the three cameras on Spider Legs, manipulating the remote controls to test the device's full visual range. All was well as Terry steered the gangly machine past the edge of the parking lot, over a log berm, up a hill strewn with pine needles. But suddenly the pictures were askew, jiggling, locked on the same patch of landscape.

Dreyfus grumbled, got up, and headed for the door.

As he came out the door of the motel, he could see Spider Legs at the far end of the parking lot, stuck and flailing. On a not-very-big hill. Dreyfus crossed to the gathered scientists.

"What's the problem this time?" Dreyfus said.

"No problem," Terry said, climbing the hill after the recalcitrant machine. Once again, he gave Spider Legs a good swift kick in the rear and, presto, he was working again. Everybody laughed. Except Dreyfus.

"If that thing's going to keep screwing up," he said, "I don't want it up there."

"The problem is ELF here," Terry said, giving the oblong box on the robot's back a nudge. It was NASA's extra-low-frequency transmitter, the device that could transmit through rocks and was destined to probe the interior of Mars. "I'm gonna fix this once and for all," he said. "Everyone turn around. Go on, turn around . . . don't look."

Everyone turned around briefly, except Dreyfus. They all turned back to watch Terry pull a wrench from his jacket and start removing the small but heavy transmitter from the robot's back.

"Just don't forget to put the damned thing back on

before NASA finds out," Dreyfus said. Question of much-needed funding, after all.

Terry removed the ELF, stashed it in a box. Nancy took it away.

Terry patted the slimmed-down Spider Legs. "So what do you say, big guy? Ready to see the sights?"

28

The whole team minus Harry and Terry were huddled around the video monitors at the motel headquarters. It was time for Spider Legs to put up or shut up; and putting up he was. As the team watched, video images played across the screens of the steep insides of Dante's crater, beamed back to them by the robot crawling across the jagged, cindery, partly snow-and-ice-covered terrain.

Greg was operating the robot's controls from all the way down in the motel. The scientists nodded their heads in approval.

Dreyfus spoke into a radio mike. "Coming in crystal clear," he said.

Up on the snowy mountaintop, Harry and Terry answered. They were hunched on the very rim of the crater, looking down at Spider Legs making his cumbersome way several hundred yards below.

On an outcropping up next to them, Harry and Terry had installed a microwave satellite antenna so that Spider Legs could transmit pictures back to Dreyfus.

Harry and Terry were smiling, encouraged as they watched Spider Legs churning away down below. Removing the ELF had apparently done the trick.

"Terry," Dreyfus said through his headphones, "it finally looks as if he's working okay."

"Man oh man, look at him go," Terry said. "Lost those twenty-five pounds of ugly fat. Never even thought about Jenny Craig."

Two of the reasons it was Spider Legs trudging down there in the crater and not Terry and Harry were the obvious danger of plumes of superheated steam venting from fissures, and the danger of lava erupting suddenly while men were walking the dome, the thin crust of hardened basalt covering the lake of magma. A third reason lay in the gases that had to be sampled and analyzed, most of which were unfriendly to man: chlorine, sulfur dioxide, fluorine, and concentrated carbon dioxide, among others.

Harry and the team especially needed to be able to track the changes in the composition of vented gases. If heavier gases like sulfur dioxide predominated, that meant the reservoir of magma beneath the volcano was relatively old, sluggish, and less likely to erupt. But if lighter, more volatile gases like water vapor and carbon dioxide started showing up in quantity, that indicated the arrival of fresh magma under pressure. Fresh magma was the free-flowing, surging, dangerous stuff that could turn Dante's Peak into Dante's Inferno at any time.

Below in the crater, as if to test the mettle of his handlers, Spider Legs crapped out again. The same thing that had happened before—upper frame extended, legs flailing. Clearly something other than the ELF's extra weight was wrong, some design flaw they had not perceived.

"Great, just great," Terry said, reaching for a gas mask and starting to move toward the edge of the cliff. "Here we go again."

Terry was about to confront a fourth reason why only robots, and not humans, should mess around in the craters of live volcanoes.

In the temporary observatory, Dreyfus and Nancy shook their heads as they watched the monitors.

"Terry's masterpiece is a piece of junk," Dreyfus said.

Behind them on the long table, seismograph needles were jumping around. The array of little jugs that Harry had buried all over Dante's Peak were dutifully sending back signals of increasing underground activity.

Nobody was watching. They were all transfixed by the now static images of terrain coming from the robot's three cameras, and waiting for pictures of Terry climbing down from above.

Harry stood watching from the crater's lip as Terry descended the steep, slippery side of the bowl toward the spot where Spider Legs had crapped out. He proceeded with great care, peering out of a bulky gas mask equipped with a microphone and transmitter.

The embankment grew even more sheer, and the trail to Spider Legs led under a sharp overhang of rock.

Terry reached the robot where he was stuck and flailing. It was right at the edge of an inner crater. He gave him a swift kick.

Spider Legs started to walk. Terry threw his hands in the air triumphantly. Harry smiled. Then Spider Legs stopped again. Inexplicably.

Terry mumbled into the mike, "I think he's purposely trying to piss me off."

"Terry," Harry said, "maybe you should forget Spider Legs and get back up."

Forget his baby? Terry ignored that bit of advice and started climbing down toward Spider Legs. He was grumbling. "For the four hundred and fifty thousand bucks this thing cost us," he said, "it oughta be able to stand on its goddamned head and fart 'The Star-Spangled Banner.'"

Harry, though he smiled at Terry's quip, was uneasy. "Just be careful down there, Terry," he said. "Don't be a cowboy."

At the temporary observatory, everybody was glued to the monitors. Then Nancy, her back stiffening, straightened up to stretch. She glanced over at the seismographs.

"Paul?" she said. "Something's going on."

Dreyfus spun around and took a look at the seismograph needles jumping around. Activity, yes, but not severe. A judgment call. He said to Stan, "What do you think?"

"They're minor quakes," Stan said. "Micros."

What they couldn't see from the angles provided by

the three cameras aboard Spider Legs was the rock overhang, the heavy basalt outcropping looming above Terry and Spider Legs.

Dreyfus, still undecided, reached for the mike. "Maybe I should tell them to call it a day," he mused aloud. "Harry?" he said into the mike. "Harry?"

No reply.

Harry, trying to keep sight of Terry, was moving sideways along the rim of the crater, jostling and causing static in his headphones. Terry, below, was moving directly under the outcropping of rock, bending toward Spider Legs.

Harry spoke into his mike: "What was that, Paul? I didn't catch you."

At that instant, an earthquake—a *small* earthquake—shook the crater.

It was just big enough to dislodge the outcropping of rocks and ice over Terry's head. Terry only had time to look up as it collapsed and he disappeared beneath the rubble. Spider Legs went flying, two of its cameras smashed.

Up on the rim of crater, Harry screamed into his radio. "Terry! . . . Terry!"

All they could see on the monitors at the motel was a kaleidoscopic jumble of falling rocks, flashes of light, and patches of darkness as Spider Legs took the hit and tumbled.

29

Because Spider Legs was lying on his side with only one operative camera, the picture he transmitted back was at a crazy angle, all askew. And what Dreyfus, Nancy, and Greg could see from that point on was severely limited. It was just enough to let them know that Terry was in trouble.

Dreyfus barked into the mike: "Harry, what's going on?"

Harry was moving sideways along the rim, staring into the dusty chaos below, hoping for a glimpse of Terry and Spider Legs.

"Get that chopper up here," he screamed into the mike. "Now!"

Just then the ground gave another small tremor and more rocks tumbled down below.

Harry turned from the crater and scrambled down

the rock slope toward the staging area in the rear where he and Terry had stowed their packs and tools.

Down in the temporary observatory, Stan was already on the phone to the chopper pilot.

Dreyfus shouted into his mike. "Harry?" he said. "Harry, goddamn it!" Harry wasn't answering. Another wave of blinding dust blew across the robot's remaining eye, blanking out the monitor. Dreyfus slammed the mike down in exasperation.

Stan held his hand over the phone and shouted to Dreyfus: "Sonuvabitch pilot wants to renegotiate his rate!"

"Just give him whatever he wants!" Dreyfus shouted back.

Stan went back to the phone and gave the pilot Hutcherson his price, then ordered him into the air instantly. Stan couldn't blame the guy: he knew volcanoes, had seen the death and havoc Mount St. Helens had wrought. One's livelihood and life were on the line every time he flew anywhere near an active volcano.

"Look!" Nancy said.

Harry appeared in the side-tipped image on the monitor. He was climbing down toward Spider Legs— toward where they assumed Terry was trapped. He had a hand radio with him and a rope over his shoulders.

"Crazy lunatic is gonna get himself killed," Greg said.

"Is that chopper on its way?" Dreyfus asked anxiously.

As they watched the monitor, Harry moved out of

frame. They could see nothing but a crazy angle of the caldera as the dust slowly cleared.

On the mountain, Harry clambered down and across a sheer slope where the footing was perilous; it was especially hard to navigate with his visibility impaired by the gas mask. As he moved gingerly to where Terry was pinned down, another small temblor sent a cascade of rock and rubble bouncing down. Harry had to dive into a fold in the rocks to dodge huge glancing boulders.

He inched forward, waiting for the dust to clear. He was just above the original pile of rubble. He could see a bit of Terry's loud, ugly shirt in between the chunks of ice and rock. Terry's gas mask lay beside him. The man wasn't moving.

Harry finally made it down to Terry and started cautiously clearing away the debris. Terry's eyes opened.

"Didn't tear the shirt, did I?" he said mischievously.

Harry grinned sardonically. "Unfortunately not," he said. Then he stopped grinning. Terry's leg, which he had just uncovered, was at an impossible angle.

Harry picked up his radio.

At the temporary observatory, Dreyfus and the others perked up as the radio crackled.

"Terry's broken his leg," came Harry's voice. "We're going to need some help up here."

Dreyfus and the team gritted their teeth. Here was the worst part of this long-distance setup. There was little they could do now but offer encouragement and keep their fingers crossed.

"Hang in there," Stan said. "The bird is on the way."

• • •

As Harry cleared the remaining debris off Terry, he could hear the welcome sound of the helicopter approaching.

The bird came into view above the lip of the crater. It looped out over the central dome and eased down toward them at an angle. But not too low. It stopped its descent and hovered high overhead, blowing the snow and dust around. A cable snaked out of the ship and eased down toward Harry and Terry, a safety harness dangling from the end of it.

"Hang on, Terry," Harry said. "Almost home." He clicked on his radio mike. Patched through the motel transceiver, his voice went right to the pilot.

"Lower," Harry said, "Lower . . . another four feet."

The pilot barked into his radio: "This is as close as I get."

Harry jerked his head up toward the chopper. "Lower, goddamnit!!"

In the helicopter, the pilot gave the finger to the radio. His rotor blades were already close enough to the sidewall that any weird downdraft or microburst would bring him crashing down. "For what you're paying this is as close as I get."

"Get down here, you sonuvabitch!" Harry screamed. "Or I swear to God, I will personally rip your heart out."

The pilot muttered to himself. With extreme caution, watching the rock sidewall like a hawk, he dropped the extra few feet.

Harry jerked the harness, wrestling it around Terry's

body. Then before locking it, he disengaged the rope from his shoulders and looped it into the harness.

Blind to all Harry's actions and the helicopter's maneuvers, Dreyfus and the others below could only wonder. "What the hell is going on up there?" Dreyfus murmured. The monitor showed only an expanse of empty crater in front of the robot's one good eye. On the radio they heard the loud whump-whump-whump of the chopper and over it, Harry's occasional grunts.

The pilot was not doing a good job of keeping the harness steady, and Terry was being dragged. Harry screamed into mike: "Hold it steady, for Christ sakes!"

Simultaneous with his words, a fumarole—a white-hot ejection of gas and steam—shot up out of the ground at the near edge of the dome, about eight feet away from them.

Terry, in a blissful state of shock, said, "Pretty cool, huh?"

Harry ignored it and struggled with the rope and the not-yet-secured harness, trying desperately to loop the rope around his own waist and arms. "DOWN! GOD-DAMN IT!" he screamed. "DOWN!"

The pilot, watching steam and gas spew up at high pressure toward him from the fumarole, shouted back, "HELL NO! YOU CAN COME UP HERE AND KICK ASS ALL YOU WANT TO BUT THERE IS NO WAY I'M GOING ANYWHERE NEAR THAT."

At the temporary observatory, they were glued to the monitor and tearing their hair out, hoping for enough of a glimpse to tell them what was happening. They heard the roar of the copter engine go up in pitch and grow louder.

As the pilot throttled up to escape the threat, the scientists below be damned, Harry tightened the loops on his rope and lunged toward Terry. At the same moment the fumarole vented again, and a second one near it opened and spewed.

The monitor in the temporary observatory was completely obscured by the steam from the fumaroles. Nobody could see a goddamned thing. Then through the billowing steam . . .

Harry and Terry appeared on the monitor, rising up together on the cable, being whisked off by the helicopter. Terry was dangling by the rescue sling and Harry from the rope below him.

Dreyfus, Nancy, Stan, and Greg couldn't believe their eyes. They smiled. Dreyfus chuckled. "Sonuvabitch," he said. "He did it."

An observer watching Dante's Peak from a distance would have seen the strange sight of a chopper rising out of a caldera with two men twisting on a line below then the two men being slowly winched up into the chopper as it churned away from the danger zone.

30

At the ranger station helipad, word had gotten around and a crowd, including Rachel, had gathered to meet the helicopter.

Pilot Hutcherson had radioed ahead once he got Terry and Harry on board, reporting Terry's condition and requesting that an ambulance be waiting.

Now, as soon as Hutcherson put the bird down, he ripped his shoulder harness and headphones off and shot out of the cockpit. Without a word to anybody he steamed across the highway to the Golden Teapot Bar & Grill. He needed a couple of stiff ones. His nerves sure weren't what they used to be, twenty-five years ago, when he was flying gunships in and out of hot zones in Vietnam.

EMTs got Terry on a gurney and wheeled him away, Harry by his side. Onlookers patted Harry's back, congratulated him, wished them both well. As the EMTs loaded Terry into the ambulance, he grinned up at Harry. "Tell the truth, Harry," he said. "You got a buzz offa that too, didn't you?" Terry laughed.

Harry patted his arm but didn't reply. The ambulance doors closed and the vehicle pulled away.

Rachel appeared at Harry's side. "Are you okay?" she said.

Harry looked at her. It was clear she had been crying. "Yeah, Rachel," he said. "I'm okay." They held a look.

Then Harry saw Dreyfus pull up in the USGS van.

"Excuse me," Harry said. He went straight to Dreyfus, who smiled at him.

"Great job, Harry," he said.

"Paul," Harry said, low but with urgency on his voice, "there's a hell of a lot of activity up there. You'd better call a meeting, put the town on notice."

Dreyfus's smile disappeared. "Harry," he said, annoyed, "I know it was pretty intense up there, but I am not going to start a panic because of a few minor tectonic quakes."

" 'Minor?' " Harry said in disbelief.

"The biggest quake we saw," Dreyfus said, "was only a two point nine and—"

Harry was getting angry. "I don't give a damn if it was a one point one," he interrupted.

Dreyfus put a hand on his arm. This is what he was afraid of—Harry flipping out, going overboard, running on emotion rather than reasoned judgment. "Harry—" he began to say.

"Those quakes were shallow, Paul," Harry said,

interrupting him once more. "Damned shallow. I was up there. I felt them."

"You don't—" Dreyfus began again.

Harry cut in forcefully. "And they weren't tectonic," he said, "they were magmatic."

Meaning these weren't seismic shocks coming from deep in the subduction zone down in the earth's crust, but that they came from the movement of magma welling up within the cavities of Dante's Peak itself. "I'm telling you, Paul," he said with certainty, "there's magma rising. I think it's going to blow."

The argument had gotten the attention of several onlookers. Dreyfus lowered his voice, glared at Harry.

Dreyfus gestured for him to keep it down. "I'm warning you, Harry," he said, "I will not have one of my people scaring the hell out of everybody with guesswork and hunches."

"This isn't a hunch, Paul!" Harry said. "There are fresh cracks up there and the snow's starting to melt. We have to—"

Dreyfus decided enough was enough. He went for the stopper. "I am not going to destroy the credibility of the United States Geological Survey because you've got a guilty conscience."

Harry was stunned. "What?" he said. Had he heard Dreyfus right?

"Needlessly evacuating Dante's Peak is not going to change what happened at Galeras," Dreyfus said. "It's not going to bring back Marianne."

Harry reacted with fury. He was right in Dreyfus's face. "This isn't about Galeras," he said. "This is about Mammoth, isn't it, Paul?"

"Mammoth?" Dreyfus said.

"You're prepared to risk the lives of thousands of people," Harry said, "because you're afraid of us calling another one wrong."

The rest of the team had congregated nearby and were listening to every word. Now Greg leaned into the pissing match and pulled Harry back. "Easy, Harry," he said.

Dreyfus was livid—being called afraid! He was afraid of nothing. He had responsibilities; he had to use judgment. Getting in a punch-up over this issue—with Harry, of all people—was worse than pointless. It undermined his authority. He stopped the argument cold. Turning to the others, he announced: "Another forty-eight hours ought to tell the story." He wheeled around and walked away.

Harry ground his teeth and muttered to himself, "Sonuvabitch."

31

In the little community hospital on a wooded hillside just west of town, Terry had a sunny room with a view of the scenic mountains. There in the distance was the magnificent snowcapped cone of Dante's Peak, looking as though it had been placed there by God solely for man's aesthetic pleasure.

Harry, Nancy, Greg, and Stan were visiting Terry in his bed. They took turns signing the cast on his leg. Everybody was laughing, joking.

Except Harry.

"Doc says I can leave as soon as they make sure my head is okay," Terry said, with a grin that said he knew what a setup line it was.

"See you in ten years," Nancy said.

They all laughed, Terry the hardest.

"The truth is, Terry," Nancy said, "I think Spider

131

Legs was just getting even with you for all those kicks in the butt you gave him."

Again laughter from all but Harry.

He was preoccupied, staring out the window at Dante's Peak. He was trying not to obsess, trying to be as blithe, cool, and professional about the situation as the others. But every way he turned it, it still looked dangerous, threatening. Not something to be cool about.

"Listen," he blurted, "you guys are going to have to help me convince Paul that this mountain means business."

That was a conversation stopper. They all looked at each other, then at him.

"Harry," Greg said finally, "I hate to agree with Paul, but there's no real evidence to suggest that anything weird is going on up there. It's just like Mount Baker back in the seventies, and there was no eruption then."

Nancy shrugged her agreement.

Craggy, gnarled Mount Baker, some two hundred miles to the north, was the northernmost of the Cascade volcanoes, within hailing distance of the Canadian border. *Koma Kulshan*, the early Native Americans called it—"the Broken One"—after an eruption blew off part of its summit. It blew its top again in 1843, sputtered for the next forty years, then went to sleep for almost a century.

In March 1975 it yawned and appeared to be awakening. It sent up formidable clouds of steam in a towering white plume, and began to produce more than a ton of sulfurous gases every hour, making for poor breathing for many miles around.

The USGS sent an earlier version of its SWAT team hustling up there (most of the present crew was still in high school or grade school). The white plume began to darken with quantities of volcanic ash, and the geologists were ready to sound the horn that Mount Baker was about to go into full eruption.

They quickly discovered, however, that the temperature of the venting steam was only about the boiling point of water, not the 220-plus-degree steam that results from water meeting up with fresh flowing magma in a volcano about to erupt. They concluded that Mount Baker was just acting like a sauna, blowing off surface water that had seeped down to hot rocks deep below the surface.

And they were right. The steam bath was all that happened. The mountain subsided again into its long sleep.

Harry knew all about that—this was different. "You were down in the town," he said, annoyed. "I was up there; I know what we saw."

They turned their heads toward Terry. "Don't look at me," he said. "All I saw was a pile of rocks on my head. Oh, and some pretty cool gas jets."

"Without enough sulfur dioxide content to worry about," Greg said gently to Harry.

Harry didn't say anything for a moment. Then: "My ninth-grade science teacher once told me that if you take a frog and throw it into boiling water, it will jump right out . . . but if you put in cold water and heat it

133

up gradually, it will just sit there until it slowly boils to death."

"What's that," Nancy said, "your recipe for frog soup?"

"It's my recipe for disaster," Harry said. "If we'd just gotten here today—now—we'd know we were in hot water and we'd put this town on alert."

Another heavy silence.

Finally Terry spoke. "Say, Harry?" he said. "What happens if you take a duck and throw the duck into a pot of boiling water?"

"You get duck soup," Greg said.

"Or a horse, Harry?" Nancy gibed. "What if you throw a horse in boiling water?"

They were all enjoying themselves at Harry's expense. Harry forced a smile.

32

In the town of Dante's Peak, no news was good news. The volcano was sending out no bulletins and neither were its designated watchers, the USGS geologists.

Les Worrell had managed to ease Elliot Blair's concerns and had him just about back in the corral. City council members Mary Kelly and Norman Gates were speaking to Rachel again, coming by the cafe for discreet updates—all of which were positive. Antique furniture dealer Karen Pope, also a city council member, was feeling reassured that her shop and the town would continue to be there, and so had gone ahead and paid her lease for the coming quarter and gotten the early-bird discount.

Motel owner Cluster was happy enough to actually smile now and then. The USGS team had been there a good three and a half weeks, regularly paying their bills with that guaranteed government credit card. They were bringing him and the town money, and not, contrary to the early rumors, bad news— exploding-volcano news à la Mount St. Helens. These geology wonks could keep their rooms and their temporary observatory in his conference room forever, as far as he was concerned.

But it wasn't to be.

Harry, Dreyfus, and the team were gathered in their headquarters checking out the latest data from the seismographs, tilt meters, and strain gauges. Greg was logging in the most recent COSPEC gas readings. Spread all over a large worktable were the infrared satellite heat photos they'd been receiving via modem.

Terry was back at work with crutches and a cast on his leg, a new loud shirt on his bulky frame. He was studying the figures from the laser gun they'd set up to calibrate changes in the mountain's size. "Steady as a rock," he said.

"Been that way all week," Dreyfus said to Harry.

"There's been no harmonic tremor," Stan said.

"And neither the laser nor the tilt meters show any change in the mountain's shape," Terry said.

"I think we've seen all this big baby's gonna do," Nancy said.

Dreyfus turned to Harry. "The mountain's wired," he said. "Our equipment's in place. We can keep an eye on things from home base in Vancouver from now on. Our work is finished here."

Harry reacted. "I think we ought to at least give it another few days," Harry said.

Dreyfus had already made up his mind. His tone

136

said: Forget about arguing, I'm past that. "I promised you two days and I gave it a week," he said. Turning to the rest of the team, he announced: "First thing in the morning, we're out of here."

The rest of the team nodded in professional agreement. But they were disappointed. They hated going back to their mostly paperwork jobs down in Vancouver. Nancy especially was disappointed to be leaving, but for reasons closer to Harry's. The more years she spent as a volcanologist, the more she became convinced it wasn't all science, that it was part art and instinct.

There was something about the swarming microquakes here that she couldn't put her finger on. That and the pattern of carbon dioxide release made her silently agree with Harry that there might be more going on than met the eye of the instruments.

But she kept her own counsel; all she really had to offer was instinct.

Then again, instinct had served Nancy well in pursuit of the one other great passion of her life: horses.

Horses had been what she was all about from the time she was eight years old. She had her own quarter horse on the family farm in Iowa. She taught riding in the summers at the country club and worked as a groom in the stables at the state fair racetrack. At one point she seriously considered becoming a trainer.

Her strength with horses was her innate understanding, her ability to tune in to what was going on with them by watching their behavior. And to communicate through murmurs and body movements rather than the whip and the shout. She read their health and emotional needs with her hands and her heart. She was a natural.

Nancy was well into a joint science/pre–veterinary medicine major at the University of Iowa when she abruptly fell in love with boys. Crazily in love. That pushed the horses—and the vet career—off center stage. She found herself in career limbo.

But even as horses had moved her in a primal way as a girl, excited her with their power—and even as men did, too, for a while—she knew she would always look for the same kind of excitement in a career.

She considered working toward being an astronaut; the thought of the visceral excitement of being hurled into space by the roaring shuttle boosters was catnip to her.

But it turned out there was excitement closer to home.

A big square-jawed flashing-eyed professor picked her up at a faculty-student cocktail party and on the walk home swept her into an embrace behind a rose-garlanded campus gazebo. It was a thrillingly dangerous beginning to a three-year live-in affair. He, it turned out, was a professor of geophysics, specialty volcanology.

The one maddening thing about their affair was his refusal ever to take her with him when he went on periodic on-site field trips to Central and South American volcanoes. He said it was too dangerous.

That did it. She quietly switched majors and studied to become a volcanologist in her own right.

138

Her love of volcanoes outlasted her love of the square-jawed flashing-eyed professor. The last time she saw him was at a volcano site in Mexico with a pretty, wide-eyed graduate student hanging on his every word. It was Harry who grabbed her arm and stopped her from heaving a chunk of basalt at him.

33

Stein's Bar was packed. The clientele was in a good mood. Word had gotten around and the cloud of impending volcanic apocalypse had lifted. The prospect of prosperous times in Dante's Peak was in the air, and it gave everybody a lift.

Onstage, a Pacific Northwest version of Lou Reed was performing some talking, mumbling blues. Some bar patrons were actually listening. The rest were drinking, schmoozing, brooding, watching the pool players.

Chief Vincent sat at one end of the bar listening to the bar talk, compiling material for his *Oral History of Bars,* Cascades section.

The story he was eavesdropping on at the moment was Pete the plumber telling the bartender about his most mysterious recent case.

It seemed that the big house belonging to the retired options arbitrageur, Matthew Hale, had a case of rotating plugged drains. Every time Pete was called out to the house, a different drain had stopped running. It was baffling. Finally he hired a subcontractor to come down from Seattle with high-tech fiber-optics viewing equipment. "We looked at the obstruction and looked at it," Pete said. "Finally I said, 'That looks like an apple.' The little girl in the family said, 'Oops.' Turns out they had these fancy French toilets with big holes; the daughter had tossed an apple down one and it had been rolling around the system for weeks." Pete laughed and slapped the bar.

The bartender just shook his head; he thought he'd heard 'em all. Chief Vincent pulled his lined ledger out and started scribbling straightaway.

At a table by the front window, the investor Elliot Blair sat drinking with a happy Les Worrell. Nancy, Greg, Stan, and Terry were shooting pool.

Harry sat at a table with Rachel, sharing a bottle of wine as a good-bye drink. "Do you ever get to Vancouver or Portland?" Harry said.

"I'm usually pretty busy," Rachel said.

"What do you do for fun?" he said.

" 'Fun'—what's that?" Rachel said with a grin. "Oh, wait, I remember . . . fun's what you have when you *don't* have two kids, a business, and a town to run."

The large form of Paul Dreyfus approached from the bar. He had a stranglehold on a bottle of microbrewery beer, not his first of the evening. He was in a good mood.

"Mind if I join you?" he said to Rachel and Harry.

They gave him a friendly look.

He sat down. "Before we take off," he said, "I'd like to thank you for the hospitality, Mayor Wando."

"It was a pleasure," Rachel said with a genuine smile.

"Well, awfully nice of you to say that," Dreyfus said, "but I don't think you'll be too sorry to see us go."

Harry nodded toward Les Worrell and Blair. "Our presence here is not exactly good for business, is it?" he said.

Rachel looked at Harry. She had had the same thought, of course—often—and had wondered how it might be affecting her judgment. And for that matter, the judgment of the politically savvy Dreyfus. Were they all just engaging in wishful thinking, each for his or her own reasons?

Les Worrell spotted this friendly confab and saw an opportunity to further close the deal. He approached with Elliot Blair in tow, stopping in front of Dreyfus. "I was just reassuring Mr. Blair," he said, "that if there was anything real to worry about, you USGS guys wouldn't be pulling out tomorrow."

"Since I'm about to sink eighteen million dollars into Happyville here," Blair said, "if there's a chance that these are the last days of Pompeii, I'd like to know."

Dreyfus laughed. "Don't worry," he said. "You've got nothing to be concerned about." He turned. "Has he, Dr. Dalton?"

Harry was caught off-guard.

Les and Blair were waiting for his response.

Dreyfus smiled as he pressed. "How about it, Dr. Dalton?" he said. "Can you give these gentlemen one single, sound, incontrovertible, scientific reason why we should stick around?" He meant it. "Because if you *can,* we will." Dreyfus was certain the scientific evidence didn't add up. He was convinced Harry was going on nothing but intuition, twisted by the ghosts of his own tragic past.

Dreyfus was waiting. Les and Blair eyed him.

"No. I can't," Harry said at last.

Dreyfus smiled. He rose from his chair and made a come-along gesture to Les and Blair. "Let me buy you fellas a drink," he said, leading them off toward the bar.

Rachel smiled at Harry. "It's getting late," she said. "I have to get home to the kids."

"I'll walk you," Harry said.

As they headed toward the door, Terry looked up from the pool table and called out: "Hey, Harry, wanna play?" He was teasing. He saw the situation.

Harry waved him off and walked out the door with Rachel.

Greg grinned. "He's busy," he said. He proceeded to line up his shot. "Eight ball in the end," he said. He hit it just hard enough and it ran true the length of the table. Game to Greg.

"I'm tired of this game," Nancy said, scooping up the cue ball. "I want a drink." She tossed the cue ball in the air once, caught it, and plunked it down on the "break" spot at the end of the table. Then she, Greg, Stan, and Terry on his crutches walked to the bar.

What none of the team saw as they left the pool table

was what the cue ball did next. It started very slowly to roll away from the spot at a weird, impossible, curving angle.

Up at Mirror Lake, where Rachel's ex-mother-in-law was living her lonely life in peace, not a single light disturbed the night, and the black water was so still it reflected individual stars.

Out in the middle of the lake, there was a sudden disturbance. Several huge bubbles rose slowly to the surface and burst. Acid bubbles. Then a fountain of small bubbles. Then the lake was calm again.

Until in the same patch of water something silvery arose. A fish. A dead fish. Then more and more, until the surface was glittering with dozens of dead fish.

34

It was a beautiful starry night. Rachel and Harry walked down the quiet main street, then across the bridge on the way to Rachel's house.

"What time are you going tomorrow?" Rachel said.

"Six A.M.," Harry said.

"I wish you weren't leaving," she said matter-of-factly.

"Don't worry," Harry said. "Dreyfus is right: We can keep an eye on the mountain from Vancouver. I guess we don't really need to be here anymore."

Rachel smiled sadly and said, "I still wish you weren't leaving."

Harry took her hand and they stopped walking and looked into each other's eyes. They were about to kiss.

Then headlights appeared. A car drove over the bridge. Rachel quickly dropped Harry's hand and moved away. The lady driver slowed the car and smiled as she passed.

"Evening, Rachel," she said.

Rachel waved. Then she looked back at Harry, who obviously wanted to kiss her. But Rachel chickened out and started walking.

"Jeannie Lane," she said. "That'll give her something to talk about for at least a couple of weeks."

Harry grinned. "Oh, at least," he said. He joined her and they continued walking over the bridge toward Rachel's house.

Rachel's house was dark when they got there, but for some lights in the living room. Maggie, the teenaged baby-sitter, was hunched in a beanbag chair reading *Les Miserables* for school, trying not to fall asleep. She stretched and got up when they came in.

Rachel smiled and got out her wallet to pay her. "Are they sleeping?" she said.

"Sure are," Maggie said.

"You free Saturday night?" Rachel said, paying her.

"Saturday early I have chorus, but I'll be done by about eight," Maggie said, collecting her book and her issues of *YM* and *Seventeen* from the floor.

"That's fine," Rachel said. She walked the girl to the front door and let her out. "Good night," she called after her.

She shut the door and turned to Harry. They were suddenly a bit tentative around each other, both feeling about the age of the teenager who'd just walked out the door.

"You want some coffee or . . . ," she said, uncertain.

Harry took her in his arms. "No, Rachel," he said, "but thanks anyway." He was about to kiss her when an approaching car threw light up through the window and seemed to stop right outside, breaking the moment. The car sped up and went on by, but it was too late.

Rachel's emotions were suddenly rising in a way that took her back fifteen years. "I really think we ought to have some coffee," she said, jittery.

But Harry didn't let her go. "I don't know how to tell you this," Harry said. "I've never really cared for your coffee."

They smiled at each other. His face was coming closer.

Rachel felt herself trembling. She was amazed. "It's been a long time since I've been with anybody," she said, her eyes widening.

"Same here," Harry said. "But they say it's like riding a bicycle . . . once you learn—"

"—you never forget," Rachel said with a smile, beginning to relax into his arms. Just as Harry was about to kiss her Lauren's voice trailed out from the hallway. "Mommy?" she called, "Mommy, is that you?"

Rachel moved back from Harry, calling out to her, "Coming, Lauren." She smiled ruefully at Harry and went down the hall to the bedroom.

Lauren was half sitting up in bed. She smiled sleepily at her mother. "I'm thirsty," she said.

"Okay, sweetheart," Rachel said, giving the girl a kiss and pulling her blankets up.

She went back into the hall and past the living room, headed for the kitchen sink. She whispered to Harry, "I think she'll fall right back to sleep."

In the kitchen Rachel picked up a glass and turned on the water. "Oh, dear God in heaven," she said softly to herself, "*please,* let her fall right back to sleep." Then she peered at the water and said in surprise, "Yech . . . what's happened to the water?"

"What is it?" Harry said, appearing in the doorway.

Rachel showed him the glass of water. The water was brown and murky. "Must be a broken pipe," she said, "or—"

Harry grabbed the glass of murky water out of her hand. He smelled it.

"What is it?" Rachel said.

Harry was holding the water up to the light, examining the particles suspended in it. "Where's the town's water supply come from?" he said.

"It's about five miles away," she said, gesturing in the direction of the backcountry toward the big mountain.

"We have to get over there," Harry said with stony urgency.

Lauren appeared in the doorway, rubbing her eyes. "Where's my water?" she said.

35

In Graham's bedroom, Rachel stood over the bed of the groggy, half-awake fourteen-year-old.

"But I don't want to take a ride," he said. What was with his mother? It was the middle of the night. What was Harry doing there? Lemme go back to sleep, he thought.

Harry stood in the doorway holding Lauren's hand. Lauren was wide awake, already dressed in a jacket over her pj's.

Graham tried to turn over. Rachel whipped the covers off the bed. Direct-action time. Rachel was used to getting kids to move when they had to. Graham gazed up at her in wonder, sensing something wrong. He started to wake up in a hurry.

•   •   •

The ride up the mountain was carried out in silence. Harry was resolved not to cry wolf, and especially not to alarm the kids needlessly.

The spring water head was back in the hills, up a switchback graded dirt road built by the county public works department. It was narrow and slow going, but then Mother Nature's fresh water supply system didn't need a whole lot of maintenance in these parts.

Fresh clear water flowed year-round from many springs in the hills, fed in specific by the snowmelt off perpetually snowcapped Dante's Peak, and in general by wet weather coming in off the Pacific, rising up and over the Cascades and dumping most of its rain and snow on the western side of the mountain chain.

The trees around the springhead lit up with headlights as Rachel's blue Land Cruiser came around a bend and pulled up in the gravel and dirt turnaround. Rachel and Harry hopped out. The kids were sound asleep in the back.

Their flashlights stabbed the dark as Rachel led Harry up to the tall concrete walls which enclosed the spring water system. She unlocked the high chain-link gate and let them in.

Harry bent and illuminated the water in the wellhead with his flashlight. He shined the light at different angles, then lifted a handful and let it fall. No question about it: The water was muddy, darkly polluted. Harry moved along the side of the pool toward the damp, echoing interior where the water entered. He got down on his hands and knees and smelled. His expression was grim.

Rachel noticed it now. "What's that smell?" she

150

said. Dante's Peak water never smelled; the purity of its water was a material factor in the town's winning the livability award.

"Sulfur dioxide," Harry said. "As magma forces its way up into the substrata, mud works its way into the water table. We saw the same thing at Mount Pinatubo in the Philippines."

Mount Pinatubo rang a bell with Rachel. She remembered: a Philippines volcano that erupted recently. "What does it mean?" she asked.

Harry shook his head in regret. Here we go again, he thought. He tried to think of a softer way of saying it but couldn't. "This mountain is a bomb, Rachel," he said. "And its fuse is getting shorter."

36

It was the middle of the night. All quiet in the town. Not a soul stirring at Cluster's Motel, least of all Paul Dreyfus. Harry stepped up to his door and banged on it.

Dreyfus was sound asleep. Harry banged again, harder. "Wake up, Paul," he called. "Wake up!" He steeled himself; this wasn't going to be easy.

Dreyfus staggered out of bed and opened the door to Harry. His look said, This better be incredibly good, or you're going to be missing your head.

"I've got that scientific proof you wanted," Harry said, and started into the room past Dreyfus.

"What the hell—" Dreyfus said.

Harry pushed past him and went right to the bathroom sink. He turned on the water, gestured Dreyfus to come look. The water was dark and muddy. Dreyfus reacted with puzzled dismay.

"I just came back from the town's water supply back in the hills," Harry said. "It's the same."

Harry held a glass of murky water up to the light for Dreyfus to examine.

"Oh my God," Dreyfus said quietly.

The whole team had been up and cracking for hours in the temporary observatory as day broke. Dreyfus was on the phone. Harry, Nancy, Terry, and Stan were checking the seismographs, the tilt-meter and strain-gauge readings, and the remote gas sensors. Greg was at the satellite station charting temperature changes.

"The quakes are coming in swarms now," Harry announced. "Another two point four."

"Gas readings are going up, too," Stan said.

"Picture a guy, he's been constipated for about ten years," Nancy said, bent over comparing seismometer readings across different sectors of the cone, "and he's just eaten seventeen bad chili dogs." She looked up and grinned. "El Bufadoro!"

Dreyfus, speaking into the phone, said, "Thank you, Governor. Good-bye." He hung up the phone, then turned to the others and announced grimly, "The National Guard will be here by midnight."

He sounded resolute and sure, but in truth, Dreyfus had the cold sweats. He was committed now, and he felt he was doing the right thing. But the memory of the Mammoth debacle haunted him. If the same thing happened here—a big fizzle—he could kiss his director's job good-bye. He'd be back burying seismometer jugs on routine surveillance calls.

At the same time he was hoping for a big fizzle, for the sake of the good people he had come to know in this town.

The volcanologist's dilemma.

Stan called over to Harry, "How much time do you think we've got?"

"There's just no way to tell for sure," Harry said, looking now at Dreyfus, at the strained look on his face.

A moment passed during which Dreyfus met Harry's gaze and held it. Finally he gave the slightest of nods, silently acknowledging that Harry had apparently been right all along.

"Harry," Dreyfus said, "have Mayor Wando put the town on alert."

Harry grabbed up the phone.

37

The local TV station was a tiny one-room studio. One camera, hardly any equipment. It was used to broadcast regular monthly city council meetings, a local cooking show, a garden show, a tool show, area ski and road reports in the winter, and a rundown of international lumber and mineral prices. Its regular broadcast day began at noon and ran three hours.

This day Rachel preempted all regular programming and got on the air herself at noon sharp.

Harry was standing by watching as Rachel spoke into the camera.

". . . in response to the potential volcanic threat to Dante's Peak, I am requesting that all residents attend a public meeting at the high school at six P.M. to discuss the evacuation of our town."

•   •   •

In the front office at his motel, Cluster, watching Rachel on TV, went white.

"A representative of the United States Geological Survey will be on hand to explain the facts to you in detail," Rachel continued. "This is not the time to panic, but everyone should realize the threat is real. The USGS people are here to give us the benefit of their considerable experience in such situations. Let me reemphasize: Don't act rashly; come and get the facts."

Cluster was terrified. He rushed out of the room and into the temporary observatory, where Dreyfus and the team were closely monitoring the fast-evolving situation.

"When's the mountain gonna blow?" Cluster said. "Tonight, tomorrow? Is it going to get this far? How much time have we got?"

Dreyfus and the team exchanged looks.

"Whoa . . . slow down," Dreyfus said. "There's nothing to get alarmed about yet. We just want to be prepared."

The look on Cluster's face said, Bull! What are you keeping from me? What are you hiding?

Dreyfus gave him a reassuring smile. "We'll let you know the minute we know anything," Dreyfus said.

On the main street of town, heads turned as the sheriff's patrol car cruised by. Through the loudspeaker, the sheriff announced the news.

"Attention, all citizens," said the amplified voice. "There will be a meeting held in the high school

156

gymnasium at six P.M. to discuss the evacuation of Dante's Peak. To repeat . . ."

The people along the street turned as one and stared up at Dante's Peak. Sure enough, rising above it, almost invisible against the gray sky, was a grayish plume. Not big; but any plume at all from the sleeping behemoth was sufficient to strike terror into their hearts. Why hadn't they noticed it before?!

The ever-practical plumber, Pete Prugo, turned his pickup on a dime and headed for the gas station.

Karen Pope stood with her hands on her hips, furious. She had just paid three months ahead on her store lease!

Tony the barber herded his customers back into their chairs. Known for his fast haircuts, he bore down. His swift scissors started flying more furiously than ever.

Chief Vincent listened carefully to the announcement, watched the plume for a minute, then wheeled his bicycle across the street to G. G. Farber's bicycle shop. He asked Greasy Guy—the town's affectionate nickname for the usually grime-covered owner—for the biggest rear-wheel luggage rack he had in stock. Greasy Guy smiled his distracted smile and agreed to install it right away.

Chief Vincent stepped outside and took another look at the mountain. Then he stripped off his coat, draped it over his arm, and carefully weighed himself on the sidewalk scale. He stepped off the scale, put his coat back on, and walked away in a hurry.

Santiago the gardener, cutting the lawn at Matt Hale's big house on the hill, heard the announcement from a distance. Santiago was an elfin, earnest man from Zaratecao in the landlocked heart of Mexico. He was extremely conscientious about his work. Now he dropped everything and ran for his battered little pickup truck, intending to fly home. He had a wife, Elsa, and four babies—too many, he knew, but what was life without kids?

Then he stopped himself, his sense of responsibility getting the better of him. He turned back to finish the work he had promised. He watched the smoking mountain the whole while, sweating.

38

The Blue Moon Cafe had been busy all afternoon, with customers coming in and out—not ordering much, just checking that the cafe was still there, Rachel was at the helm, and all continued to be more or less right with their world.

And was there any news? For most people, it wasn't quite sinking in.

Rachel repeated her TV warning over and over: Take it seriously, start thinking evacuation, and come to the school for the meeting.

Nearing six o'clock, the cafe was almost empty, and Rachel was on the telephone at the end of the counter.

Harry had just come in to get her, and slid onto a stool to wait. Graham and Lauren fidgeted on nearby stools, watching their mother.

"Ruth, please . . . ," Rachel said, low, so her voice

wouldn't carry to the half dozen patrons still in the place. "You have to come down from there. Harry says the mountain could blow up anytime and—"

"That's his opinion," Ruth said, from her sound and secure log bungalow on Mirror Lake.

"Let me try," Harry said, taking the phone. "Hi, Ruth. Harry Dalton," he said. "Listen, Ruth, this situation has become quite serious, and I think you better consider—"

"I'm not leaving and that's that," Ruth said into the phone. She was looking out her living room window as she spoke—across the lawn, across the placid lake to the beautiful forested mountains rising grandly in the clear afternoon air. She was so emotionally locked into this place she could not imagine turning her back on it and leaving. What life she had remaining to her was here. Death, she thought defiantly, would be preferable to displacement.

"Ruth, really—" Harry's voice went on over the phone.

But Ruth hung up. Gazing out on the vista, her mind wandering back to the early years of her marriage, to those times of intense happiness as she raised her son in this idyllic splendor, she did not see the signs of impending destruction lying out there in plain sight. Ruth's mind was clear with a thousand details of the beloved long-ago, but her eyes were not what they used to be . . .

". . . Hello? Hello?" Harry said into the phone down at the cafe. "She hung up on me," he said to Rachel.

Rachel grabbed the phone from Harry and quickly

redialed. She grumbled to herself, "Come on, Ruth. Pick it up. Pick it up!"

Graham was worried. "She's not coming down, is she?" he said.

Rachel waited and waited, then hung up the phone and turned to face her worried children. "If Grandma wants to stay up there, that is her choice. There's nothing we can do."

"But Mom—" Graham said.

Rachel had on her drill instructor expression. "Kids," she said. "Home. Now. And I want you packed up and ready to go as soon as I get back." She stooped and took her fourteen-year-old by the shoulders. "Graham, you're responsible now," she said. "Look after your little sister."

Then she and Harry were out the door.

Graham got up and held out his hand for Lauren to take. "Come on, pickle puss," he said.

"Oh, okay, chu-chu face," Lauren said, hopping off her stool, refusing his hand, following him out the door.

39

The usual late-day chill swept over the town of
Dante's Peak as a huge orange sun fell into the
grape-hued mountains to the west. The clouds rising
over the Cascades were stained purple and gold like a
bruise. It was a stunning sunset, the likes of which
occurred only a few times a year and were supposed to
portend fine, balmy days to come.

A few stragglers hustled into the high school gym
through the double doors under the banner HOME OF THE
MINERS.

Rachel, on the stage with a microphone, was winding up her brief remarks. Harry was up on the stage
too, along with the sheriff and the head of the water
department, each waiting his turn to address the
gymful of people.

". . . I know it's tough to think about leaving our homes," Rachel continued. "But it's the responsible thing to do right now. And if nothing happens, well, it's better to be safe than sorry."

A clamor rose up as people turned to their neighbors and exclaimed and compared notes. Some in the crowd had heard enough and started toward the doors.

Susan, a young nurse-trainee at the county home for the aging, stood up near the front. "Do we have to wait?" she said loudly, above the noise. "I mean, if we want to leave now?"

The crowd quieted.

"Of course you don't have to wait, Susan," Rachel said. "You can leave whenever you want."

Susan smiled, kind of embarrassed, and sat down.

Elliot Blair, seated right up near the front so as to get the full picture, had got it, in Kodacolor. He stage-whispered to Les, "I'm getting out of here before it all hits the fan." He rose and walked down the aisle and straight out the door.

Dr. Fox turned to Les Worrell, who was dour-faced with regret as he watched Blair leave. "There goes your pension, Les," she said.

Les gave her an acid look and got up and followed Blair out, looking down at the floor the whole way out. That's the story of my life, he was thinking; if I call my broker tomorrow and tell him to put it all on Microsoft—Boom! They'll go bankrupt.

"Will our homes and shops be protected if we leave?" Karen Pope called out. "What's to prevent looting?"

"The National Guard has already been alerted," Rachel said. "They'll be here by midnight."

Rachel saw a break between questions and turned. "Now, I'd like to turn this meeting over to Dr. Harry Dalton," she said.

Harry stepped up to the podium and took the microphone. He looked out at all the upturned faces. It was no longer just an anonymous crowd to him—he knew too many names, too many identities.

"I want to make it clear," he said in strong tones, "that these are just precautionary measures. We don't want to start a—"

The ice in the water jug on the table in front of Harry rattled. His eyes riveted on it. He continued quietly, almost to himself, "—panic."

The building shook. Just a tremor, but enough to get the notice of this ever-more-tense audience.

At the temporary observatory, Terry looked up from some papers, puzzled. "Did anyone feel that?" he said.

Dreyfus looked around nervously.

They had been recording swarms of miniquakes all day, but only the kind that dogs and hypersensitive seismometers can pick up.

In the gym, people started to murmur uneasily. Just then there was another small rolling tremor.

"Everyone please stay calm," Harry said. "We'll all be okay if we keep our heads. Now, starting with the people nearest to the exits . . . let's move out quietly."

Another tremor hit. This one was bigger.

Someone screamed. Suddenly panic began spreading like wildfire. People bolted for the doors.

The basketball hoops swung wildly. A banner fell from the rafters.

40

In the conference room at Cluster's Motel, the windows rattled and Dreyfus stood straight up. "I felt *that*!" he said.

The whole team moved to the instrument tables. A riot of new data scrambled across the seismographs and computer monitors.

The first panicked people burst through the front doors of the high school. They ran into the middle of the street and looked up at Dante's Peak, glowing a rosy color in the warm, direct light of the late-day sun. Above the distant cone, a gray plume boiled high into the sky. No more white venting steam. This was a cloud of volcanic gases and ash.

•   •   •

At Rachel's house, Graham ran out onto the verandah after the two noticeable quakes. He took one look at the mountain and rushed back inside.

He ran through the house yelling, "Lauren!! The mountain's blowing up!!!" He bolted down the hallway and yanked open her door. "Lauren," he said to her, out of breath, "listen, forget packing. Here—" He grabbed her coat, tossed it to her. "We gotta do something. Come on." He dragged her out and down the hall.

The people still inside the high school gym were the unlucky ones. As more tremors hit, the yelling and confusion mounted. In the melee, children were separated from their parents. Screams of "Mommy!" and "Daddy!" and children's names echoed off the cinderblock walls. An old man went down under the feet of the stampeding crowd.

At the temporary observatory, Dreyfus peered at a strain-gauge monitor. The graphics were going berserk. He looked down the line of five seismographs. "Nancy, look at this, look at the progression in these," he said, then looked up, "and feel that." The building was vibrating, thrumming. "These are harmonic tremors, eruption tremors. Magma moving."

Another series of vibrations hit.

"Why look at instruments when you can look at the real thing?" Nancy said. She rushed out. The others followed.

Outside in the gravel parking lot, Dreyfus and company stared up in awe at the smoking mountain.

"Will you look at that . . . ," Nancy said.

Dreyfus and company watched the mountain, transfixed. What gripped them most was the dark color of the plume. Mount St. Helens had similarly started rattling windows in neighboring communities, but her crater activity was limited to nominal bursts of white steam at low temperature for many days, and it took her another seven weeks to develop more threatening signs and then erupt.

Here the dark plume rising out of Dante's Peak meant there was already lava ash being ejected. It meant that approaching the surface was fresh magma charged with much hotter steam, and the steam was escaping from the magma, coughing out ominous clouds of lava ash with it.

That in itself was not a problem. If all the steam bubbled out this way in small coughs, the eruption would be a quiet and gentle affair with perhaps a tongue of lava flowing meekly out of the crater.

The dangerous possibility was that the magma rising to the surface and throwing off this early ash was the thick, viscous sort that didn't give off its steam easily. This viscous kind of magma absorbed a great deal of water and rose to the surface with a heavy charge of steam trapped inside the gooey melted rock.

Not ordinary steam, either—steam superheated to above 750 degrees centigrade, and under colossal pressure seeking release. This was the megaton charge behind volcanic violence. If Dante's Peak was this sort of volcano—and there was no way of knowing while the magma was still in the ground—it could explode like a nuclear bomb and blast cubic miles of thick lava and poison gases far and wide.

Whichever kind it was, it was showing signs of reaching critical mass far faster than Mount St. Helens had.

"Looks to me like it's about to blow its top," Nancy said.

Another shock wave hit. The motel sign fell in a shower of sparks.

"Code Red if I ever saw one," Dreyfus said. "Twenty-four hours or less."

41

Still in the high school gym, Harry was trying to make sure everyone was safely out. He fought his way through the panicky citizens toward the fallen old man. He helped the man up and steadied him on his way to the door.

Rachel was right behind him, reuniting Jeannie Lane with her two scared children.

"Harry!" Rachel called. "I've got to get the kids!"

The sound of glass exploding outside echoed in the nearly empty gym. Harry and Rachel hurried out with the crowd. The crush of people exiting the school had been too much for the plate glass windows in the entrance hall—one of them exploded outward and people fell into the street.

Panicking, terrified people completely blocked the exit.

"This way," Rachel said, starting down the hall the other way. Another long tremor and tiles fell from the ceiling in a cloud of dust and debris. Rachel tripped and fell. Harry dragged her to her feet and they managed to exit the building through a side door.

Rachel and Harry ran around the side of the school. They saw the mountain and stopped to stare at it, stunned.

Great clouds of ash billowed up from its peak. The ground shook and there was a deep low rumble.

"Oh my God," she said, "you were right."

Suddenly, the steeple of the church across the road began to topple. People screamed and tried to scramble clear as it fell, crushing an empty school bus parked beside the church.

People were jumping in their cars and trying to drive off all at once. They pulled out from parking places without looking, cutting each off, bending fenders. Two cars smashed into one another as Rachel and Harry ran toward his Suburban.

A little girl stood there holding a kitten. She was crying amidst the confusion.

Rachel looked at her, slowed.

"Better come on," Harry called, unlocking his truck.

Rachel saw the little girl's mother coming. She waved, caught the mother's attention, and pushed the little girl in her direction. She turned and ran for Harry's truck.

The USGS team was hurriedly dismantling the temporary observatory, packing much of their expensive equipment back into the boxes and foam-lined cases.

They left two seismographs and some other monitoring equipment wired up and running.

Dreyfus was on the phone yelling at an official on the other end of the line. Even among the hardened field scientists, a low level of panic and shock had set in, so fast had this eruption come on.

"We're being hit hard by a series of quakes," Dreyfus barked into the phone. "We can't wait until tonight. We need the Guard here now!"

On the monitor in front of him, a satellite photo scrolled down, showing a vast ash cloud already stretching far to the southeast. One of the remaining seismographs showed almost continuous quakes.

The main road in town was crawling with cars. Harry nosed the Suburban out onto it from the side road where the high school sat.

Now the earthquakes were coming hard on top of each other and were even more severe. Everything Harry and Rachel could see through the windshield looked blurred, there was so much ground vibration.

A power pole fell, sending sparks flying as Harry horsed the Suburban out of the way.

At the far end of town, cars swarmed up onto the elevated highway that led past town. Straining under the stress of the quakes, a section of the entrance road to the highway collapsed, then part of the highway itself. A speeding car tumbled off the fractured pavement. A following big-rig fell off, too. A neon sign fell onto the trapped cars.

With Rachel directing him, Harry swerved down a side street and detoured onto a less-traveled back street where the traffic was ragged and erratic. Rachel looked out the window up at the mountain, still glowing in the last rays of the day's sunlight.

It gleamed like a beacon above the peaceful suburban houses, but it spewed inky clouds of volcanic ash.

Harry picked up his car radio mike.

"Anybody there?" he said into the mike. "Paul?"

At the motel conference room, Dreyfus hit the key on the radio. "Harry, Harry, I hear you," he said. "Where are you?"

Harry talked on the radio as he one-handedly swerved the truck around a retaining wall that collapsed into the street. He made no effort to hide the fact that he was deeply angry that they were all in this harrowing situation. He had vowed that it would never happen again; that those he loved would never be exposed to this kind of avoidable danger.

"I'm driving Rachel to her place to get her kids," he said, none too friendly. "Soon as I'm done I'll be back to help you pack out of there."

Dreyfus picked up on his tone—there was no way not to. "Harry, for whatever it's worth," he said, "you were right and I was wrong. I'm sorry." It was all he could do. If he could go back and have another shot at it, he would.

"See you soon, Paul," Harry said, and signed off.

42

Quakes were really swarming now, and not micro-quakes either.

A line of cars was trying to snake onto the raised highway past the overturned car and big-rig and the fallen sign. Without warning, the town hall collapsed on top of several of the cars, effectively cutting off that way out of town. The rest of the cars scrambled to turn around and find another escape.

Tony the barber was finally closing up his shop when Chief Vincent hurried in. He didn't want a haircut, he wanted his stash: three cloth-backed ledgers he had stored for safekeeping on a shelf in Tony's supply room. Volumes 8, 9, and 17 of *The Oral History of Bars*. With a nod of thanks to Tony he hurried out—and headed down the street to a bookstore where he was pretty sure he had stashed a couple more volumes.

In the Suburban, Harry and Rachel drove back onto the main street and headed toward the bridge separating this commercial stretch from Cluster's Motel and Rachel's neighborhood. Through the windshield they could see Sheriff Turner out of his patrol car directing traffic, trying to make some sort of order out of all the chaos.

The ground under the town was shaking like a sorting table at a fruit-wholesaling business. Not one quake after another, just constant vibration.

Harry and Rachel approached the bank building. Traffic completely blocked the street. The building began to collapse, then crumbled in a cloud of dust like a cartoon building. It pitched forward, burying a passing car.

Flying rubble barely missed the Suburban as Harry cranked the wheel hard into an alley and sped down it, seeking an unblocked route to Rachel's house.

Transformers exploded around them and fires burned as they roared through the alley.

The bridge was going to be a problem, Rachel had warned him.

It was. Traffic had built up and jammed, choking the road leading up to the bridge. Just as the Suburban was about to join the jam, one of the pumps at the gas station at the intersection exploded into flames. Cars backed hurriedly away.

Harry floored it through the momentary opening and zipped across the bridge. In seconds he was on the road leading to Rachel's place.

Overhead, the mountain continued to spew tons of black ash into the air. It was beginning to settle on the town like a fine, greasy black rain, covering all surfaces.

Car paint distributor Dick Boyd, heading home in his cherry red MG, saw the gray ash settling on his car's new paint job and saw what havoc the stuff was going to wreak with car finishes. Canny entrepreneur, he saw opportunity in duress. It took him just a minute to hop out and stick his business cards in the windshield wipers of a whole line of ash-covered cars.

As Boyd got back in his car to go home and get his wife and two kids, Warren Cluster roared past with his young son and his doper ex-wife in the car, headed out of town. Cluster had left the motel wide open and just fled. His ex-wife looked stone cold sober and petrified.

Harry's Suburban skidded to a halt in front of Rachel's place. Rachel saw what was wrong instantly. "My truck's gone!" she said.

Harry and Rachel leapt out and ran inside.

"Graham!!! Lauren!!!" she yelled, fearing the worst.

Up on the mountain, on a winding road dark with late-day shadows, Rachel's Land Cruiser roared along. Inside, Graham drove as Lauren peered desperately ahead through the windshield. The truck slewed toward an abrupt edge. Graham fought it back onto the road.

43

Rachel bolted into Graham's bedroom, looking around frantically. She pounced on the handwritten note at the foot of the bed. She was reading Graham's scrawl as Harry came through the door.

"Oh my God!" she said. It was worse than she'd expected. She looked at Harry. "They've gone up the mountain to get their grandma!!" she said, fear running up her back like an animal.

Harry and Rachel ran out of the house and leapt into the Suburban. They sped down the street and were about to turn toward the town when Harry slowed the truck and looked up at the bridge in the gathering dusk. It was choked to a standstill with traffic.

He looked up and down the swift-running mountain river. If anything, it looked higher to Harry now than it had before. Which could mean the volcano had been heating up for a while already—literally. Hot magma nearing the surface would have been melting the ice and snow around the peak, sending more water into the runoff system that ended up in the several snow-melt rivers like this one.

"Any other way back across the river?" Harry said.

Rachel looked at him in anguish. "No!" she said.

Harry dropped the Suburban into gear and took off. Dust and gravel flew as he turned the truck away from the bridge, shot across the road, and headed straight down the bank toward the river.

"Are you out of your head?" Rachel said, holding on for dear life.

The truck rocketed straight into the river in a massive spray of water. And then kept on going.

It moved out into the flow downstream from the bridge—into the fast-running current in the broad heart of the river. The water rose up to the Suburban's hood. The sturdy vehicle kept on churning.

Upstream near the bridge, the driver of a Volvo sedan on the far shore, waiting to try to squeeze onto the bridge, saw the Suburban apparently fording the river with ease. If they could do it so could he, the driver decided. He took off down the bank into the water. Another car followed.

These cars were not equipped to ford a river. They nosed into the onrushing water, drove ten or fifteen feet, and stalled out. Quickly, they were picked up and spun by the strong current. They began to float downstream.

Inside the Suburban, Rachel watched in fear and wonder as they moved deeper into the river and water began to lap at the windows. Miraculously the Suburban seemed right at home. Which it was, with the engine's snorkel feeding air to the motor and the upraised tailpipe reaching well out of the water, throwing exhaust into the air.

They were three-quarters of the way across and gaining steadily on the far bank when Rachel turned her head and saw something that made her heart leap. Coming straight toward them were the two floating cars. The water was too deep for Harry to do any fast maneuvering. He barely had more control than the runaways.

"Hang on!!!" Harry said.

SLAM! One of the cars whacked into them hard. The Suburban swerved, wavered, and found its little bit of traction again.

The other car, the Volvo, bounced off them too and was carried like so much driftwood down the river. One after the other, the terrified drivers jumped out of their cars and swam for it.

The Suburban got more traction and headed for the far bank. A second pump at the burning gas station exploded in the background as Harry drove up out of the river.

The Suburban found the roadway and started racing through the town. Behind them, one of the underground gasoline storage tanks at the gas station, all but empty except for fumes, exploded like a bomb. Parts of the station's metal superstructure rained down on the street three blocks away.

44

The Land Cruiser climbed up the mountain toward Mirror Lake. Graham, at the wheel, concentrated hard to keep his mother's truck on the treacherous winding road.

Lauren, in the seat next to him, hung on to the dash and leaned up close to the windshield. The falling ash made it almost impossible to see even in the daylight, and now night was coming on.

"Maybe you ought to turn on the lights," Lauren said.

"They are on," Graham said.

"How about the windshield wipers?" Lauren said.

Graham thought about that. "I don't know how they work," he said.

"I'll find them," Lauren said, moving toward the

steering column. Graham moved her back with his knee.

"Come on," he said. "Don't fool around down there . . . you'll mess something up."

"Like what?" she said.

"I don't know," he said. "Something." The truth was, he was really scared. Lauren could feel it, and that scared her even more.

There was a rolling jolt and Graham tried to steer to keep them on the road. This unnerved him even more—he knew he hadn't hit anything. And the road was moving. The earth was shaking like a wet dog.

Boulders crashed down onto the road ahead of them.

Somehow—through blind luck or Ruth's secret driving lessons—Graham managed to keep the truck on the road while jerking the wheel to the right, then left, moving around the boulders.

As they rolled on toward the next curve, where the road narrowed and the ground fell sharply away on the right-hand side, Lauren said in a small voice, "Maybe this wasn't such a good idea."

In the Suburban, Rachel, thinking what a bad, bad idea her kids had had, was punching numbers on the cell phone, trying to call ahead to Ruth at the lodge. She got a *"We're sorry—all circuits are busy—please try your call again later . . ."* message.

"Damnit," she said. She tried again. She got the same message.

At the temporary observatory, Nancy and the rest of the team were still monitoring instruments and recording data. Nobody had even suggested leaving yet; this was an invaluable opportunity to plot the curve from early danger signs to eruption, all accordioned into a few weeks and now a few hours. They could come out with a prediction profile that would set a new standard.

Greg was crouched at the computer, just finishing entering data from all the seismometers, tilt meters, and strain gauges in one program. The computer was integrating it into a three-dimensional rotating graphic. Greg could now see a computer-animated picture of the column of magma rising within the volcano.

He called the team over. They whistled and let out low exclamations. As the graphic turned, they could see that a large mass of magma was intruding into the southwest flank of Dante's Peak near the summit. If it continued in that way, one of the real possibilities was a violent eruption whose main force would hurtle debris roughly in the direction of the town.

They looked at one another, evaluating this new information.

While most residents of Dante's Peak were in their cars choking the roads out of town, a crowd was gathering at the city parking lot just across the street from Cluster's Motel.

The rumor was, a helicopter was coming to take people out.

Now the people could hear its roar in the night sky. Its xenon landing light flashed on. In moments it settled down out of the dark into the pool of light cast by the streetlamps surrounding the lot. For-hire pilot Hutcherson brought his rent-a-bird in to a soft landing.

People took cover from the dust and grit thrown up

by the downdraft from the rotors. As soon as the copter was on the ground, they rushed forward, opened the doors, and tried to dive in.

Across the street, Nancy jumped to the window, drawn there by the whump-whump-whump of the arriving copter. She stared across at the people massing around the bird and clambering aboard.

"Uh-oh," she said. "Looks like our asshole pilot plans on flying people out of here!"

Dreyfus came to the window to look out. "Jesus," he said. "If he sucks any ash into his engine, he's had it. Doesn't he know?"

Dreyfus charged out the conference room door.

The chopper pilot was barring the helicopter door to most of the people, letting on a select few who were obviously paying. He made a quick count—the chopper was already overcrowded with people, sagging on its landing struts. He slammed the bay door shut.

In the front seat, Elliot Blair peeled off bill after bill for Hutcherson from a thick wad as the pilot strapped himself into his seat. Les Worrell handed over a fistful of cash from the backseat. Hutcherson stuffed the cash in his flight jacket and started to wind up the 1,400-horsepower Lycoming turbine for takeoff.

Dreyfus ran out of the motel and across the road just as the engine reached a high whine. One man, hurrying away from the parking lot, passed Dreyfus. "He's getting fifteen thousand a pop," the man said. "Cash only."

Dreyfus waved frantically to the pilot. "STOP! . . . STOP!!" he yelled. "Goddamn it . . ." But it was too late. His voice was lost in the noise of the chopper's takeoff. He stood, his hair blasted back by the down-draft. "Don't try it," he said almost to himself, watching the copter rise into the ash-laden sky. He threw his hands up in despair.

45

The pilot took the helicopter up at a steep angle away from the wires of the town. As soon as he had minimal altitude, he banked back to cross over the town, meaning to head down through the deepest cut between mountains. It was a pass that took them along the flank of Dante's Peak, briefly, on their way to open air.

The crowd of anxious passengers peered out at their damaged city and made ready to breathe a sigh of relief. But ironically, breathing itself was suddenly an issue; fumes coming in from the gases in the air made them cough and choke.

"This as fast as you can go?" Blair said as the copter labored at a very low altitude over the shops and houses.

"We've got twelve people in here. We're heavy,"

Hutcherson said testily. "You don't want to . . . OH DEAR JESUS!"

The tail of a huge, black, falling plume of ash whipped down off the mountain, microbursting off the ground right in front of them, then billowing back up. They were going to fly right through it.

"What?!" Les said, staring into the murk. "What is it?"

"Shut up! I can't think!" the pilot said as he jammed at every control in front of him, putting the copter into a hard bank away from the roiling ash cloud.

But to no avail. The blades cut into the ash storm, the stuff was ingested into the turbine, and it sputtered and coughed and died. Then, terrifying silence.

A look of horror spread across Hutcherson's face, his hands frozen on the controls. The helicopter floated for an endless beat. Then screams ripped the air as it started to sink.

The rotors freewheeled, parachuting the machine, slowing the descent a little—but just a little. It was too heavy; too many passengers. It fell straight down out of the sky, fast, struts first, but with no control over where it would land.

Harry had just turned the Suburban onto the road on the outskirts of town that led up through the pass to Mirror Lake. He looked up and jammed the brakes in reflex as the helicopter plummeted right toward them.

The copter slammed into the hillside in front of them, cartwheeled past them across the road into a warehouse below, and exploded in a ball of fire on impact.

A horrifying sight. No one in the chopper could have possibly survived.

The Suburban skidded to a halt, and Harry and Rachel looked back at the inferno. "Oh my God," Rachel said.

The flames reflected off Harry's face. "Where are we?" Harry said, grabbing up the mike.

"Top of Exeter Street," Rachel said.

Harry spoke into the mike. "Can anyone hear me?" he said. "A chopper's gone down! It's on Exeter Street at the edge of town. Get the fire services up here!"

At the temporary observatory, the team spun toward the radio and grimaced at the bad news. They had seen it coming. All those people . . .

"Okay, Harry," Stan said into the mike. "We copy."

Harry hooked the mike back on its hook, staring out at the fiery wreckage. "There's nothing we can do," he said. "We've got to get your kids." He stepped on the accelerator, taking them away from the burning wreckage and up the mountain.

Harry grabbed the mike again. "Rachel's kids are headed up the mountain. We're going to get them."

Back at the temporary observatory, the team exchanged grave looks as they listened to Harry's words and looked at the seismographs and the computer screen showing the animated magma rising.

"He's crazy," Greg said in a hushed voice. "He doesn't have enough time."

Stan leaned into the mike: "Harry, listen, we don't think you have enough time."

They waited. No answer. They stared at the computerized rendering of the invading mass of magma inside Dante's Peak. Maybe it would stop rising and just crystallize quietly at depth, letting its steam charge out little by little.

Maybe. But not likely, given its behavior so far.

Most likely it would pull a Mount St. Helens. But less powerful, of course, they told themselves.

Mount St. Helens was an order of magnitude rare in modern times—a magma-steam explosion equivalent to twenty-one thousand atomic bombs of the Hiroshima class. When Mount St. Helens blew, it expelled magma, rock, and ash out horizontally at a speed of five hundred miles an hour. The steam venting from the red-hot magma was hot enough to glow in the dark as a flame.

They could only hope that such an explosion, or even a fraction of such an explosion, would not occur while Harry, or any of them, were within ten miles of that mountain.

46

The lights were on at Ruth's lodge as the Land Cruiser pulled to a skidding, sliding halt in front of it. The vehicle headlights barely cut through the murk, reflecting back thick ashy air. Inside the snug lodge, Ruth was apparently going on with her life as though all was normal.

The kids jumped out, both of them shouting, "Grandma! Grandma!"

Ruth rushed out the front door with Roughy, extremely surprised to see her grandchildren. "What are you doing here?" she asked, giving each of them a hug.

"Grandma," Lauren said, "we came to get you and Roughy out."

"What?!" Ruth said.

"Get in the truck, Grandma," Graham said, tugging her by the hand.

"You drove up here?" Ruth said. "All by yourselves?"

"We had to," Graham said.

"Your mother is going to kill you," Ruth said. And me, she thought.

A jagged tremor hit, and Roughy yelped and bolted, right past Graham and off into the woods beside the lodge.

"Roughy!" Ruth called, upset. "Roughy!" She started after the dog.

Harry raced the Suburban up the mountain road.

"It's not far now," Rachel said, grim-faced.

Harry hit a straight stretch and accelerated—just as the ground buckled in front of them. The Suburban bounced and bucked like a bronco, and was just getting out of the bad patch when—

SLAM!

A rock slide on the slope above them dislodged a tree. It came crashing across the road. Other boulders crashed down onto the road ahead of them.

Harry reacted instinctively, pulling the Suburban up on the shoulder, punching the gas, powering around the obstruction. As he fishtailed back onto the roadway and saw clear sailing ahead, more trouble arrived behind them. Big trouble.

A piece of the mountain far above them, a huge projecting section of granite rockface, had been vibrating with the repeated tremors and was weakening with each one. It now lost its grip. The whole face of the mountain gave way and slid. It came slamming down on the road, obliterating it. There was no way back down the mountain.

Rachel looked back, saw the vast dust rising above the landslide, and knew that they were trapped. She turned to Harry with a look of utter dismay. Then bit her lip, trying not to let the dire implications overwhelm her. Her kids were going to need her and Harry. They were going to get out of this.

In the dark woods, breathing the repulsive thick air, Lauren and Graham tried to keep up with their grandmother as they all shouted Roughy's name.

Finally Ruth, exhausted and out of breath, stopped yelling. And what she then heard on the foul air brought her up short—her grandchildren's sweet, young, strong voices yelling for the old dog. They were babies. They had whole lives to live. This wild-goose chase for Roughy was placing them in jeopardy. She snapped out of her self-absorbed fog.

Lauren and Graham were loping along in the woods on either side of her, calling frantically for Roughy.

"Grandma, do you see her?" Lauren called.

Ruth called back, "We've got to get back. Now."

"But we can't leave her—" Lauren said, turning toward her grandmother.

Ruth's face had taken on a different look, one Lauren and Graham had rarely seen. "I said, now!" Ruth snapped, holding out her hands for the children to take. She turned with them and started marching back through the woods.

At the same moment, Harry and Rachel in the

Suburban were approaching the dirt road that led to the lake and the lodge. Rachel shouted, pointing out the turn: "There!"

Harry braked hard, slid some yards, cranked the wheel, and pulled the truck off the mountain road down the dirt drive toward Ruth's.

He slalomed down the rutted path and skidded to a halt in front of the lighted lodge. He stuffed the radio in his pocket, and he and Rachel jumped out. He switched on the powerful flashlight in his hand.

They ran past Rachel's Land Cruiser, Rachel yelling, "Graham! Lauren!" They stopped when they saw the open front door of the lodge.

Only silence greeted them. Rachel's heart sank.

She had begun to try to formulate where they could be, how she could get to them, when Ruth and the children emerged from the woods. No Roughy, but the kids and Ruth looked fine.

Harry smiled. Tears of joy streamed down Rachel's face as she ran to embrace her children. She held on to them tightly as she said to Graham, "Oh, I'm just so mad at you."

"I'm sorry, Mom," Graham said, but still with that touch of attitude. He had a teenage boy's hatred of being wrong, of having to apologize. He was only doing what he had to do! he thought. But he was smart enough not to say it.

"It's not just Graham's fault," Lauren said. "It was my idea, too."

Rachel stood up and released her kids. She glared straight at Ruth.

"Stop looking at me like it's my fault, because it's

not," Ruth said testily. "Now just take the kids, get back in your truck, and go home." She refused to be taken to task by this woman. This woman who she felt was the cause of her son's running off, leaving the area, abandoning *her,* his own mother. She could not forgive Rachel for that.

"We would go if we could, Ruth," Rachel said, "but the entire road's just been wiped out behind us."

Ruth's eyes flashed with alarm—for her grandchildren.

"I swear to God, Ruth," Rachel said through clenched teeth, "if anything happens to my children because of your stupid, irresponsible attitude, I'll—"

Ruth stood her ground, albeit defensively. "I didn't tell them to come up here," she said. "This isn't my fault."

"They're here because they love you," Rachel said. "And if anything does happen to them you better believe it's your fault."

"Please, Grandma," Graham said, taking her hand. "You've got to come with us."

Ruth looked at her grandchildren. She had a tough decision to make.

Then, reluctantly, she relented. She started quickly toward the house.

"I've got to pack up a few things," she said over her shoulder.

Harry called after her, "Well, make it fast. We've got to get down off this mountain." He looked up at the belching cone of Dante's Peak. Among the billows of black ash were streaks of steam shooting up, glowing in the dark like flame.

47

In the pine-paneled conference room at Cluster's Motel, Dreyfus and the team members were still manning the instruments, but they were exhausted, everyone fraying around the edges.

Greg tried a hopeful tack. "Plenty of minor eruptions early," he said, "and tapering off now."

"Maybe we're over the hump," Stan said, picking up the theme.

Nancy looked at them like they were both crazy, and tapped the screen of the computer terminal showing the animated magma rising. "Get real, Beavis," she said. "She's just clearing her throat. She hasn't even started to sing yet."

Harry's voice came over the radio: "Paul, it's Harry. Anybody there?"

Dreyfus grabbed up the radio mike. "Harry, where are you?" he said.

At Ruth's lodge, the power had just gone out and Harry was speaking on his battery-powered hand transceiver. In the background, Ruth frantically went through her belongings, trying to figure out what to take. The kids lit the area with flashlights for her.

"I'm up at Mirror Lake, at the lodge," Harry said. "The road's gone. But we're all okay."

Lauren called out, "Roughy isn't!"

At the motel observatory, Dreyfus said into the radio mike, "This is building up to something catastrophic. I'll send in a chopper as soon as the wind blows the ash cloud off."

"Listen to me," Harry's voice came over the speaker, "get the hell out of there, Paul. Before it's too late. Don't wait for us."

On the last lines, Harry's voice broke up.

"Harry, can you hear me?" Dreyfus said. "Are you there, Harry?"

No answer from Harry. His transmission was lost.

"Maybe his battery went dead," Greg said, jumping to the set and twiddling knobs to try to bring Harry's signal in.

"I'm gonna stick around as long as I can," Dreyfus said grimly. "The rest of you should leave—now."

They all smiled and shook their heads no.

The truth was, their ready smiles were a kind of sham. The van was two-thirds packed, and they had been set to go for many hours—itching to go—as soon as Harry got there. However, none of them would ever pull out and leave one of their number trapped. It

195

was the unwritten code. And part of that code was putting a good front on it.

"Who'd want to walk out when God's putting on his big show?" Stan said.

"Can't get enough of this funky stuff, eh, guys?" Nancy said.

In the southwest quadrant of the crater atop Dante's Peak, a dome had been forming—a vast bulge in the rock caused by the upward welling of magma under pressure. Now the surface of the rock dome reached a critical point and a fissure opened up. A jet of bright red magma sprayed out—"lava," once it reached the air. The fissure grew wider, and a fountain, then a torrent, of lava belched out and flowed toward the rim of the crater. It dammed up there momentarily before spilling over and running down the steep side of the cone like water. A growing river of molten rock made its way down the moutainside.

At the lodge, Rachel was helping Ruth pack, trying to hurry her along. Ruth was looking at a photo of a happy young couple holding a baby. She smiled. "This was taken the summer we built this place," she said. "Brian was six months old."

Rachel was agitated to the point of distraction. To begin with, Ruth had shown her that photograph at least two dozen times as though it was the first. Secondly, they were in a hurry. This woman was going to drive her around the bend; or worse.

"There's no time for strolling down memory lane,

Ruth," Rachel said. "Just pack what you need and let's get out of here."

Ruth continued packing: selecting, rejecting; fondling favorite belongings, unable to part with them. A bronze Remington horse that had been her husband's, for example. She couldn't take it, of course. And yet . . .

Rachel looked daggers at the back of Ruth's head. Let's go! she wanted to scream.

On the mountain slope above the lodge, a river of bright red-orange lava, hissing and crackling, was coursing swiftly downward through the trees, setting everything in its path on fire—pine trees, brush, ground cover of needles and humus and fallen branches. The night lit up in eerie accompaniment to the deadly juggernaut charging headlong down the hill.

Now the lava flow appeared on the ridge behind the lodge, fed from behind by an ever-increasing cascade of the stuff. It spilled over the ridge and carved a burning path down the steep grade. At the bottom it spread out and marched on a broad front through the scrub brush toward the lake.

Ruth's beautiful log-cabin lodge got in the way.

The red-hot lava hit the stone base at the back of the lodge and flowed around the structure on both sides. It flowed across the dirt parking area and around the rust orange Suburban and the pale blue Land Cruiser. It set first the tires, then the rest of the vehicles on fire.

The people inside the lodge had no idea that the lethal fingers of the volcano had already reached this far down the mountain. They thought they still had time. . . .

48

"Come on," Harry said. "It's time we got moving."

Ruth repeated what she needed to believe. "I still believe that this mountain will never hurt us."

Rachel was absolutely at the end of her rope. She threw down the bag she'd been packing and glared at Ruth. "You're a fool," she said.

Harry looked out the window, exasperated. Didn't these women have any sense of the—

He stopped his ruminating and stared: A ribbon of glowing lava was etching the dark, flowing down the mountain, right around the side of the house.

CRASH!

Something immense smashed into the far wall of the lodge, sending shards of glass exploding inwards. The river of lava came flooding and tumbling into the lodge, crackling and hissing and setting all it touched on fire.

Harry and Rachel frantically herded the kids toward the door. Ruth struggled after them—and paused to grab her plastic garbage bag on her way out.

Once outside on the broad porch, which was now covered in several inches of ash like a ghastly gray snowfall, they saw that the bad news was getting worse. The vehicles were on fire. The crackling, scarlet snakes of lava had almost surrounded them, cutting off all their escape routes over land.

They turned toward their last remaining point of exit—the lake. Driven by the searing heat of the encroaching molten rock, they linked hands and ran together toward the lake.

On the dark skyline above them, the glow of burning trees and tumbling lava lit up the night.

They headed for the small wooden pier jutting into the lake. On either side of it, huge clouds of steam hissed up as the lava flowed down into the water, vaporizing it instantly and noisily. A small aluminum-hulled skiff rocked in the water by the dock.

Rachel looked across the dark water and pointed. "There's a fire road on the other side of the lake," she said. "Maybe we can get down to the ranger station and get help."

Harry herded the group into the boat.

Ruth took one last look back at the dark woods, searching for Roughy. Then, shaking off all thoughts of loss, and rejecting the nostalgic daze that threatened to engulf her even now, she faced forward and prepared to leave all her baggage behind.

199

In the bow, the kids faced out on the lake, beginning to feel a little safer. Then they saw the fish—hundreds of dead, floating fish.

"The fish!" Lauren cried, "They're all dead." Graham gaped in amazement.

They all got aboard, Rachel helping Ruth. Harry moved to the stern where the little Mercury outboard perched. He tipped it into the water and yanked the starter cord. It didn't turn over.

The kids, hanging over the bow, pulled back. Foul-smelling steam was rising off the water around them.

Harry gave the outboard rope another pull. Still nothing.

Ruth got up and moved Harry out of the way. "Me and this old outboard go back a ways," she said. She tweaked the choke, twiddled the throttle, then gave the starter cord an immense yank.

The motor kicked over on the first try.

Ruth settled down at the helm, kicked the engine into gear, and the little skiff moved quickly away from the shore out into the lake.

The rest of the people in the boat were all very quiet as they looked back at the lodge. The beautiful little place was now silhouetted in fire against the night. It was being consumed by hungry, leaping flames. Some parts of it were already crumbling in smoke and ash.

One of the vehicles exploded.

All the two kids could think about was Roughy. They stared at the trees all along the dark shoreline. Where was she? Alive or dead already? Trapped, or using her wily ways to race to freedom somewhere?

They whispered to each other, urging on each other the last possibility.

Ruth, guiding the boat, looked stalwartly ahead, smart enough not to turn and look at the devastation to her house. She would sail away from her life's home with its image intact in her memory. It would join the rest of her past that still lived so vividly there.

49

"Reporting live from Dante's Peak . . ."

A young woman news stringer was doing a live spot in the middle of town, framed so that there was maximum damage in the background: the fallen church steeple, several buildings on fire, the shorn end of the highway access road in the distance.

People still trying to evacuate carried flashlights and umbrellas to ward off the ash that filled the air like snow. Most had their shirts or pieces of cloth up over their faces like bandannas to stop ingesting the stuff.

". . . there's panic, chaos, devastation everywhere," the TV reporter said to the camera. "Many casualties have already occurred. The citizens of Dante's Peak have long lived in the shadow of this slumbering giant, never thinking it would—"

CRASH!!

She jumped, then shied away as a piece of masonry fell from the building she was standing next to.

She stuck the mike back in her face and went on: "That's all for now, Chuck. Reporting from Dante's Peak, this is Patty MacMillan, KQED News." She gave a brave sign-off smile, then as soon as the light on the camera went off, she ran screaming for the news van. "Oooooh, never again! Never, never, never!!!!"

As the news van snaked away between abandoned and broken-down cars and streaked for the last available down-mountain road, it joined the general exodus. The town was emptying out fast.

City council members Mary Kelly, the insurance woman, and Norman Gates, the retired CPA, were long gone. They had packed their families into the family cars—two each—and fled town as soon as they'd got the call from Rachel asking them to come on TV with her. Rachel wanted a united front when she announced the evening emergency meeting and asked for calm.

Councilpersons Kelly and Gates had been at the earlier meeting, however; they were privy to the fact that Harry had wanted the town put on alert weeks before. They didn't need to be hit over the head. They told Rachel good-bye and good luck and beat it as fast as their cars could carry them.

Dr. Fox had the same early warning, but she had a duty to stay, she felt. When the quakes and ashfall began, she set up at her office and responded to emergency calls from there. When the phones failed around nine in the evening, she stationed herself at the command post the just-arriving National Guard was setting up at the post office. Dr. Fox listened to the calls coming in on the Guard's military and police-band radios and CB transceiver. She responded when it made sense.

A broken arm down on Chelan Street: She jumped in her station wagon and sped down there and got it in an emergency splint, then sent the people on their way.

Several people with acute asthma attacks, unable to travel five feet: Dr. Fox hastened to them, gave them quick steroid shots and inhalers, allowing them to flee.

The fiery helicopter crash; there was nothing she could do.

At the big estate on the outskirts of town, retired options arbitrageur Matt Hale, a tall, quiet, athletically built man with prematurely gray hair, was still not quite ready. He was methodically making the rounds of his buildings, turning out lights, locking all the windows and doors, making his valuable property as secure as possible preparatory to departure. He had sent his family on ahead in the Range Rover. He had his own bags packed and in the open trunk of the Mercedes.

As a last task, he was piling his old mountain-climbing gear by the front door—the coils of rope, pitons, climbing boots, belaying gear. He had been a meticulous but fearless climber in his youth, assaying formidable peaks in America, Europe, and Asia. It was a part of his life he had left behind when he had a family. But the flame of vitality that burned in him when he climbed had marked his soul for life. How could he leave his gear behind? Wouldn't that be the same as admitting that part of himself was irrevocably lost?

• • •

On night-shrouded Mirror Lake, the stranded pilgrims were making slow but encouraging progress toward the far shore.

The small engine growled and waves lapped against the side of the boat. But then Harry heard another sound: a sizzling. He examined the hull, and his heart sank.

"Don't touch the water," he said. "It's acid."

"What?" Rachel said.

"The volcanic activity has turned the lake acidic," Harry said.

"Acid eats metal," Rachel said.

Lauren piped up in alarm, "Is the boat going to sink?"

"We'll be okay," Harry said, not very convincingly.

Now they realized what had been stinging their eyes: acid vapors.

Ruth continued to guide the boat toward the far shore, where they could now just make out the fire lane through the dark forest.

The aluminum hull began to seriously react to the acidic water.

A long, silent moment. Harry gazed off at the shore, assessing the distance. He looked down at the hull of the boat. It hadn't burned through yet . . . but it would soon.

The others read it in his face. The tension in the boat skyrocketed. He could hear the kids' breathing quicken. Harry knew he had to do something or they would all lose their minds.

"Ever hear of Pele, the Volcano Goddess?" Harry

said. "Legend has it that a little song will put you in good with the old girl."

Graham responded with fourteen-year-old bravado. "Our camp bus song?" he said, "I'll sing that." To the tune of the *Sesame Street* "Sunny Day" theme song, he rattled out:

> Hate this boat. How long's it gonna float?
> Don't stop now, I'm gonna puke in the bow.
> Oh, how long will it take
> Just to cross old Mirror Lake?
> Just to cross old Mirror Lake?

Everybody laughed. "Terrific," said Ruth. "Sing it again."

Graham, with Ruth and Lauren joining in, sang it again.

Then silence fell. Heavy silence. Their eyes were burning from the vapor rising off the water. Over the buzz of the little motor, they could hear the sizzle of acid eating the metal of boat.

Nobody spoke. All just too scared.

Harry pressed ahead. "So come on, another song," he said. "What's it gonna be? . . . Ah! I've got a good one . . . "Row, row, row your boat, gently down the stream. Merrily, merrily, merrily . . ."

Silence.

"Come on, Lauren," Harry said, "you know this one."

Lauren sang. Her voice was sweet and clear and frightened. Then one by one, they all joined in, singing rounds of "Row, Row, Row Your Boat." The only holdout was Graham, who clearly thought *this* was a stupid song to sing.

Harry caught his eye. Gave him a "man-to-man" glare; a time-to-suck-it-up-and-help-these-women look. Graham reluctantly joined in.

Rachel met Harry's eyes. Harry smiled.

With the volcano spewing red death above them, ash raining down all around, the little boat putt-putted across the middle of the lake with the chorus of eerily plaintive voices singing.

50

Rumbles and tremors continued unabated while National Guardsmen made their way along the streets of town, checking buildings to see who was left, who needed help. In an alley by Stein's Bar, they came across a white-bearded man wearing a golf visor, bent over a bicycle, tying two tall stacks of notebooks onto the rear luggage carrier.

It was Chief Vincent. He had finally collected all the volumes of the *Oral History* he had stashed around town, and had them lashed to his bike. He assured the guardsmen that all was well. He got on the bike and pushed off, balancing with difficulty, and wobbled off toward the last down-mountain road that was still open.

As he made the turn onto the narrow county road, a pickup truck with two young guys in it swerved onto the road from the other direction, clipped the bike rider, and just kept on going. Chief Vincent flew off the road into a culvert.

Councilwoman Karen Pope turned onto the county road at that moment in her big Ford Econoline van that she used for transporting furniture; now the van was crammed with people who needed rides. Pope, a feisty woman, saw the hit and run happen and was furious. Swearing at the runaway pickup, she braked to a stop.

Amidst a new episode of ground-shaking, she helped the bruised Chief up, dusted him off, and found the last inch of space in her vehicle for him.

As the van pulled away, Chief Vincent looked back at where his ruined bike and notebooks lay. No matter, he thought, marking the spot; he would come back for them. At that moment the hillside above the culvert gave way, burying his magnum opus. No matter, he said to himself, I *will* come back for them . . . Or maybe I won't. He faced ahead with benign aplomb.

On Mirror Lake, they were still singing—quietly, hypnotically—as if to drown out the terrible hissing sound. They were three-quarters of the way across now; just a little bit more and they would make it.

Then Harry saw what he feared most. The hull of the boat had started to burn through. Acid was seeping through cracks around the weld joints.

"Put your feet up on the benches," he said as calmly as possible.

They did.

Harry sang louder, as though to fortify the boat with sound. Rachel, catching his eye, sang too.

All of them, looking at each other, sang out—until the song became what it had obviously been all along.

A prayer. For this little boat traveling across a killer sea.

It looked now like they just might make it. They were maybe a hundred yards from shore. Only a hundred yards.

The boat was starting to sink lower into the water. Harry looked closely. The bottom of the boat was all but dissolved. Still, only a hundred yards!

"Hey. If you're scared," Graham said to his sister, "I've got something that'll keep you safe."

Lauren looked up at him through teary eyes. He reached in his pocket and offered her his quartz crystal. The one from the mine.

Lauren couldn't believe it. "I can have it?" she said.

"Yes," Graham said. He smiled as he pressed the crystal into her hand and held it.

Rachel smiled through her tears and gave silent thanks to the gods of family for this small blessing.

There was a long quiet moment as they slowly but surely drew nearer the far shore.

And then there was a very bad sound. The motor of the boat made a high whining noise as the rotor began spinning crazily in the water.

Ruth pulled the motor up out of the water to take a look at the propeller. Acid had completely eaten away the blades. She let the motor back down and turned to see where they were.

They did not have that far to go. Thirty or forty yards now and they were on solid ground.

Tantalizingly, they drifted ever closer to the shore.

So close—twenty yards, fifteen. But not close enough yet for Harry to leap out.

"Graham—give me your coat!" Harry said. "Your coat!"

Graham tugged off his jacket. Harry wrapped it around his fist and flailed it in the water, paddling, trying to inch the boat toward the shore.

Progress! They were moving. Just a few more yards . . . But the material of the jacket burned him as it dissolved. In seconds Harry jerked his hand away with a scream of pain as the acid water scorched him.

The coat sank into the lake.

They had almost reached the ramshackle old pier. Agonizingly close—but not close enough yet.

Harry leaned at full stretch from the bows, his fingers just three tantalizing inches from the wood of the pier . . .

And the boat began to drift away, backing off from the pier, the sizzle of acid a constant reminder that it would soon sink.

"No-o-o-o!" Rachel said.

Harry stood up in the bow and prepared to jump.

"Forget it, Harry," Ruth said, "you won't make it."

He tottered there, undecided; knowing she was right.

"The water isn't deep," Ruth said.

Harry looked around. And shouted: "Ruth, no!"

Ruth was climbing over the stern of the boat. Harry dived toward her, nearly tipping the boat over. He caught her and tried to haul her aboard. "Ruth, for God sakes—"

She jerked away from his grasp. And sank legs first into the fuming water, her clothes sizzling.

Rachel clutched her horrified kids.

Ruth, waist-deep in the water, was grimly silent as she gave the boat a heave and sent it careening toward the pier. Rachel grabbed the post boosted her kids out, and then scrambled out her seat, along with Harry.

The kids ran ashore as the old pier started to collapse—wood planking crumbling, posts buckling. Rachel and Harry dove after them.

Ruth, flailing her way after them, finally let out a scream of agony.

"Ruth!" Harry cried.

Her eyes were full of tears of pain as the acid water scalded her. She stumbled and splashed her way to shore.

Harry reached to haul Ruth out of the acid bath.

"Don't touch me!" she ordered. "You'll burn your-self."

She collapsed, her clothes half burned off, the exposed flesh of her legs raw.

Behind them, the boat fell apart and sank as the hot acidic water ate it through.

Spying patches of snow on the slope near the lake, Harry and Rachel ran to it, scooped up as much as they could carry, and covered Ruth's burned legs with it. The kids joined in, fetching and piling snow over the raw flesh.

"Don't worry, Grandma," Lauren said. "You'll be okay."

Rachel knelt by Ruth. Ruth's eyes flickered open. She smiled at her grandchildren as they packed her lower body with snow. "The world's first horizontal snowman!" she said, making the kids smile through their tears.

"We'll get you down, Ruth, I promise," Rachel said.

The pain kicked up a notch. Ruth closed her eyes.

Harry looked at Rachel. She turned away in anguish, fighting back sobs.

51

It was dawn—though nobody could swear to it, the sky was so dark. One National Guard unit in a Humvee patrolled the downtown streets of the nearly empty city, keeping wary eyes on the fireworks above—the volcano alternately spewing fire and billows of black ash.

Pete Prugo drove by in his plumbing truck, his wife Mary in the front with him. He was towing a small pickup truck, its bed heaped to overflowing with gardening and snow-removal tools—Santiago's tools, his livelihood. In the cab of the towed vehicle were Santiago, his wife, and their four children. Escaping this nightmare to carry on their lives and labors and baby-making elsewhere.

A second National Guard unit was making a final sweep of residential neighborhoods, calling out with a bullhorn, offering help. The guardsmen saw the gate open at the big house set back on the hillside, the Mercedes ready in the driveway, and lights still on inside the house.

They pulled over at the base of the driveway and one of them called through the bullhorn: "LEAVE THE AREA NOW. DO YOU NEED ANY HELP?"

Matt Hale stepped out of the house and waved his hands in a no-thanks manner. He gave them a salute, and they drove on. Hale turned and pulled his front door shut, testing to make sure it was locked. He went to the waiting Mercedes, but did not get in.

Instead he pulled his climbing gear out of the trunk. He draped the coiled rope over his shoulder, locked up the Mercedes, and walked down the driveway. He carefully locked the gate behind him. The last anyone saw of him, he was walking up a forested slope in the direction of the erupting volcano, adjusting his clamps and turnbuckles, readying for a major climb.

Up on the mountain, the sun struggled to cast its light through the cloud of ash spiraling into the sky.

In the half-light, Harry and Rachel had made a primitive gurney from branches of wood. Ruth lay on this as they carried her down the hill—Harry at one end, Graham and Rachel at the other. Lauren walked alongside, holding her grandmother's hand. Their descent was slow, and the constant ground shudderings and the rumblings and cracklings of the mountain were reminders of the peril that loomed so close.

Ruth could no longer suppress a groan of pain caused by the rolling, jouncing motion of the gurney.

She waved a hand weakly. "Stop," she said. "Please stop."

They lowered the gurney onto a mossy bank to take a break. Rachel bent to tend her, using a rag to try and gently cover the withering flesh of her lower body. Ruth moaned loudly. She couldn't stand anything touching her; it was agony enough just to lie on the gurney.

Lauren tried to slip the quartz crystal into Ruth's hand, but Ruth declined it. "Honey, that's so nice," she said in a feeble voice, "but you keep it for your luck. Okay?"

Lauren accepted the crystal back and dashed to help Graham who was picking up tiny handfuls of snows from the few patches scattered in the woods.

Harry did not like Ruth's pallor. He felt her hands and took her pulse. Her temperature and blood pressure were falling. He had seen people in similar states before. He was not at all confident.

"I'm sorry for what I said to you back there," Rachel said to Ruth. "I didn't mean it. I—"

"Sssh," Ruth said. "You were right: I *am* a fool."

Rachel squeezed her hand. "No," she said. Her long feud with this woman seemed so pointless now.

"But my son is the biggest fool of all," Ruth said. "He never should have run off and hurt you all like that."

Rachel broke down crying. It was the first time Ruth had ever admitted that maybe Rachel didn't just drive Brian off; that her son's leaving might not have been all Rachel's fault; that in fact, maybe Brian was the one most responsible.

"If anyone's a fool it's me," Rachel said. "Ruth, I never even gave you a chance. You saved our lives today." She sobbed helplessly.

Ruth stroked her hair.

"Hang on, Grandma," Graham said. "It's just another two miles to the ranger station."

She smiled weakly at the boy. "I haven't got another two miles in me, ace," she said. She put a hand out to both kids. "It's okay. I get to stay on my mountain."

Ruth held their hands tight and closed her eyes. She breathed deeply once, took a few shallow breaths, and then her lips parted. She gave a deep shudder and breathed for the last time.

The kids looked up at Harry. He felt for a pulse. But there was none. Rachel dropped her head on Ruth's breast.

"Grandma," Lauren whimpered. "Grandma . . ."

Harry moved to hold Graham and Lauren as they looked despairingly at death.

52

The mountain was beginning to erupt in earnest. The entire floor of the crater had become a rising, shuddering dome. Superheated steam and bluish clouds of sulfuric acid and fluorine vented from fissures with savage violence. Fountains of incandescent red lava burst constantly in different parts of the caldera, running, pooling together, building up.

The temperatures on the outside of the cone climbed and the snowpack began to melt. A long, broad ledge of ice and snow that had been building glacier-like on the southwest flank for years collapsed and liquefied in just minutes. Hot now, it coursed downward as mud-ash-cinder runoff. Sheets of it funneled into ravines that created hot mud rivers. Which grew. Lahars, they were called.

• • •

Rachel walked with Lauren along the hard-stubbled, rutted, punishing firebreak. Harry walked with Graham. It was like a hike over harsh terrain in a greasy rain, except that the rain was wet ash and noxious gases. They came to a cross break and clambered down the sheer side into a gulley that led steeply downward. Even harder going.

Above them, the snowmelt that had become a lahar was dropping in altitude a thousand feet every two minutes. It was joined at intersecting ravines by more mud-ash runoff until it became a broad, deep torrent pushing ahead of it a collection of debris. Trees and boulders being borne on the face of a mountain tsunami—a great hot slushy tidal wave. It funneled between high jagged ridges and sped up even more and roared down-mountain at the speed of a super-train.

Harry and company stumbled and slithered down the steep forest fire break in the half-dark of the blighted day. The air was thick with clouds of ash, the smell of rotten-egg gas and other sickly gases they couldn't identify. The ground rumbled beneath their feet. If there was a hell, this was surely a foretaste.

But there was the town, dimly outlined below. They were close. The town was within their grasp. It seemed.

In reality, it was still three-quarters of a mile. Over unforgiving, precipitous, shuddering ground—hard traveling even in the sweet light of a friendlier day.

Rachel gestured to their right, away from the fire-break and the steep ravine. There below they could see the ranger station. No signs of life anywhere around it. Evacuated. One utility truck remained in the compound, apparently abandoned.

Harry grasped at it, at the hope. "Maybe we can get that truck going," he said.

Suddenly in the distance they could hear the roar. Harry stopped and listened, and a look of terror flashed in his eyes. "Lahar," he said.

"What's that," Rachel said, looking up in fear.

"Snowmelt landslide," Harry said. "Deadly. Sssh—" He listened. Then relaxed a tiny bit. "That way," he said, and drew a line down the mountain to the east of them, where the roar now seemed to be heading.

A shoulder of the mountain called Recasner Ridge— for the Recasner family homestead that lay back up there in a beautiful piney glade—had shunted the lahar to the east. Now it filled an entire canyon that normally contained a creek and a dozen other mountain homesteads besides the old Recasner place.

As the lahar tore down from the mountain, it totaled these places. It picked up loose equipment, a barn, a car, a backhoe, a logger's flatbed. The thing was taking everything in its wake, pulling out trees at their roots.

It was thundering right down Five Mile Creek. Five Mile Creek broadened into the Silver River, which cut through the heart of the little city of Dante's Peak.

53

The guardsman leaned out of the Humvee and shouted at the insane people he could see through the open door at Cluster's Motel. The team at the temporary observatory was still doing business, monitoring and documenting this geological extravaganza close up.

"You people shouldn't still be here," he called. "The bridge is going to go!"

"We're with the USGS," Dreyfus called back. "We're scientists. We know what we're doing."

The rest of the team looked at him. This did not seem a brilliant remark, under the circumstances. "Screw science," Nancy said. She had the definite feeling they had pushed the envelope far enough—plenty far enough. "Let's get out of here," she said.

"We've got to get the rest of our equipment first," Dreyfus said to the guardsman.

"Hey, you're not listening," the guy said. "I have a direct order from the governor for you. Get the hell out of here. Now."

They got the message. Greg, Stan, and Nancy threw the remaining equipment in boxes and hustled them out to the van. Terry hobbled out on his crutches. Nancy ran back in, took one last look around to see if they had everything. Nothing left but piles of wastepaper and some old pizza boxes and a Kentucky Fried Chicken container.

Nancy ran for the two Humvees waiting to get them out. She jumped in the lead one, with Terry, Stan, and Greg already on board.

Dreyfus got into the USGS van. He was staring up at the fire on the mountain as he started to follow the Humvees out. He got on the radio, making one last attempt to reach Harry on the USGS frequency.

He keyed the mike. "Harry . . . Can you hear me?" he said, and listened. He raised no response "Harry . . . Harry . . . The bridge is about to go. Listen . . . we got everybody out—the whole town We got everybody." He waited again for a response Then he said softly, "Take great care, Harry. Take great care. . . ."

The two Humvees, followed by Dreyfus in the van. approached the bridge from the west. The bridge was intact, but the river was already thick with mud and badly swollen, just a few feet below the roadbed.

Approaching from the north, on an intersecting time curve, was the crest of the lahar, now broadened out and rolling down the river canyon with the force of a bomber group. It picked up and carried everything in the river plain—piers, abutments, boulders, back porches, animals.

The first thing the Humvee drivers saw when they drove out onto the bridge and jerked their heads around to see what was making that sudden roaring was a wall of hot liquid mud with large bobbing boulders, dead animals and parts of outbuildings in it, thundering right at them.

The flow beneath them was already all the way up to the bridge! And now here came—

SLAM!!!

A barn collided with the bridge! A geyser of mud, logs, and debris shot up over the side girder of the bridge and came pouring down onto the roadway.

The first Humvee, halfway across, got slammed by the mud and careened up onto two wheels, teetering before it whomped back down onto the roadway and somehow kept going.

The bridge itself was coming apart. The two central piers were undermined quickly and washed out, one after the other. The bridge sagged, its concrete roadbed cracking. . . .

Then a scream of stressed metal and shattering concrete and the entire thing gave way, torn apart by the force of all that mud and backed-up debris.

The first Humvee, containing Terry, Greg, Stan, and Nancy and some guardsmen, just managed to make it across. So did the second one, pulled up onto the bridge approach by its front-wheel drive just as the span gave way.

Dreyfus's van didn't make it.

Dreyfus didn't even have time to cry out as his van

was smashed by a wall of mud and water and went down with the bridge. It disappeared into the rampaging flow.

The team in the Humvee watched in horror.

54

Unaware of the tragedy below, Harry and the others reached the bottom of the hill. Through the trees, they could see the ranger station.

They approached it from the back. The station itself was closed and dark. Clearly deserted. But there was the one vehicle left—an old Forestry Service crew-cab pickup with a utility shell. It had been abandoned in the rush, covered inches thick with ash.

They ran to it. They all clambered in—and Harry discovered, not to his great surprise, that there were no keys in it. He dove under the dash and hot-wired the truck, twisting two wires together. The engine kicked over.

He found a gear, hit the windshield wipers, and they were on their way. The pickup rolled down toward the gates of the ranger station and the firebreak that would take them to the main road.

As they approached the gates, Harry could see they were locked in. No time for niceties: He jacked the truck into four-wheel drive, punched the accelerator, hit the gates at high speed, and barreled right through them. The truck raced up the firebreak for the road.

As they skidded and bounced along the firebreak, evidence of a new, more violent stage of eruption began raining around them. Small pieces of pumice slapped at the windows like hail.

Then the nightmare of Harry's life came at him again, shattering off the truck's hood: a volcanic bomb, the thing that had killed Marianne. Volcanic bombs were chunks of red-hot viscous magma or glowing rocks blown from the volcano with the power of a battleship's heavy guns. They arced out over the landscape like rockets, to fall and kill indiscriminately.

Another, bigger than the first, hit the hood of the pickup. And a third! Harry was sweating blood; it was all he could do to keep the vehicle on the path.

They reached a curve that would lead them onto the road. As they took the curve, a new horror loomed up. Harry slammed on the brakes. A river of partially solidified lava, two feet deep, lay across the road, creeping along like a live thing from a sci-fi movie. There were burning trees and brush on all sides, adding wood smoke to the already unbreathable air.

They stared at it as the truck idled, immobile. "Can we drive across that?" Rachel said.

"I don't know," Harry said. This was a new game even to him.

Everybody looked at him, expecting miracles. He was the expert, after all. It had to be possible. What other choice did they have?

They were about to find out. Harry backed the truck up twenty yards for added traction, jammed it into gear, and floored it.

They sped toward the barrier of smoking lava, jounced up and over the hardened edge, and went driving madly forward across the blackened tongue of stuff.

It was semisolid; it semisupported the speeding truck. But the heat was blast-furnace strength, and peeled the paint off the truck hood.

The tires caught fire. In short order they all exploded.

Pop! Pop! Pop! Pop!

The truck was driving on its rims.

The paint all over the body started to bubble. The rustproofing on the undercarriage melted away. The bare metal of the gas tank heated up, the gas inside started to vaporize, and the fuel line took in vapor instead of liquid gas. The engine started to misfire.

The truck bucked, lost momentum, slowed, and bogged down in the scalding lava, the wheels spinning. Burning shredded rubber flew everywhere.

At this moment, an astonishing sight appeared up ahead of them like a harbinger of hope.

Lauren was the first to see her. The first to shout, "Roughy!!"

Amazing. Roughy had made it down from the mountain of fire. She looked like hell—fur scorched along her back, covered in mud and volcanic ash. But she was apparently otherwise uninjured. Graham lightened up. So did Harry and Rachel.

Roughy was yelping happily, but she was on the far side of the lava flow. Yearn toward them though she might, there was no way that she could make it across to them.

Harry leaned out and called, "Stay put, girl. We're coming to get you."

Harry eased down on the accelerator, adding power to the wheels. All four of the wheels spun—mostly just the rims remained—and the truck clawed its way forward. They all leaned forward in their seats, as though fighting their way through by sheer collective willpower. Red-hot lava seared against the windows. The heat mounted steadily, punishing everybody inside.

A tongue of fresh-flowing lava appeared behind Roughy. She saw it, turned, spun around. She was trapped.

Harry spoke quietly to Rachel. "We're only going to get one chance at this," he said. "If Roughy doesn't make it in, we won't be able to go back for her. I've got to keep up our speed if we hope to get through this goop."

Rachel nodded.

Roughy yelped in pain as she got too close to the lava.

Almost incredibly, the truck wallowed through to the island of bare dirt where Roughy was. Harry didn't slow down—he didn't dare. Roughy rushed alongside the truck. Rachel threw open her door.

The kids screamed. "Come on, Roughy," Lauren said. "You can do it!"

Roughy leaped for the truck.

She didn't quite make it in, and she was about to fall out when Rachel lunged for her. Holding on to the truck with one hand, burning up from the scarlet lava only inches away, Rachel just managed to grab Roughy and hang on herself. Then she heaved the dog inside the cab as the truck rode up and over the final patch of lava.

The kids cheered.

Rachel was not exactly sure why, but tears of joy were streaming down her face. "How you doing, Roughy?" she said, nuzzling the bedraggled old mutt. "How you doing, girl?"

Harry smiled as he drove. The kids threw their arms around Roughy happily.

"Oh, Roughy," Lauren said, "did anybody ever tell you how beautiful you are?"

Everybody laughed.

After the tragedy of Ruth, it felt good to laugh. Roughy got many more pets and hugs and compliments.

55

The Forestry Service truck crawled out of the hills and bumped its way into Dante's Peak on its wheel rims.

The pilgrims looked around. This wasn't *their* Dante's Peak. A ghost town. Postwar desolation. A forsaken ruin full of fallen buildings, shattered glass, crushed cars, dangling signs. Ash blanketed everything, colored it gray, muting all sounds except the dull roar of the volcano above.

Not a soul was left in town; even the National Guard was gone. Totally evacuated.

The laughter in the truck died, changed to shocked silence as they took in the appalling reality.

Rachel looked around, stunned. "Eight years it took us to get this town on its feet," she said in a hushed voice. "You can't imagine the struggles. Fighting for

230

federal money. For state money. Trying to persuade Blair to build his factory here. And for what?"

The ash on every doorstep and lintel looked like gray snow. It was a landscape from another planet, a dream locale in *The Twilight Zone*.

Graham stared wide-eyed. Tears formed in Lauren's eyes.

The truck approached the swollen, turbulent river and the washed-out bridge and stopped.

Rachel looked at the ruins of the bridge. And the torrent of mud and logs flowing where the bridge used to be. She looked over at the collapsed access road to the state highway. "There's no other way out of town," she said.

A simple statement, but with deadly implications, especially to Harry. He looked through the windshield up at the volcano pouring an immense plume of ash three miles in the air. He felt the ground still rumbling constantly under them. That meant only one thing— magma close to the surface, still on the move, going in only one possible direction: up and out. This eruption was not on the wane. All his instincts told him the worst was yet to come.

"We've got to find shelter," he said.

"Where?" Rachel said.

Harry was at a loss. Then a really massive, rolling quake made them reel back and grab for the dash and the car walls for support.

The quartz crystal squirted from Lauren's grasp as she fell forward into the seatback, then pushed herself up. She fumbled for the crystal where she'd dropped it on the front seat, finally found it.

Harry stared at the crystal. An idea was forming. "The only chance we have of surviving this thing," he said, "is to get underground."

Graham smiled. He knew what Harry was thinking. "The mine!" he said.

Harry nodded. "I've got to make a stop first," he said, turning the semicrippled pickup around in the other direction.

As they traveled down the street, Harry gave silent thanks for this hardy vehicle. The ride was bumpy and jarring, but it was rolling shelter. It was taking them where they needed to go and keeping the ash out of their lungs.

He pulled in at Cluster's Motel. The door to the conference room/temporary observatory was wide open.

Harry climbed out of the truck. "I'll be right back," he said, and dashed from the truck into the building.

The temporary observatory was a mess. What equipment remained lay broken on the ground. He flipped a switch. There was no electricity. He looked around frantically in the dimness for something as the building shook constantly. His heart sank. The team had cleaned the place out, obviously taking with them the thing he had come after. Leaving nothing but overflowing trash receptacles, some maps and printouts on the walls, a pile of empty food containers scattered on the floor where they had fallen from a corner table.

The whole building was vibrating furiously. It felt like it was about to fall in. Harry turned for the door and started out—when it came to him. He turned back and jumped for the pile of food containers. He threw aside pizza boxes and found what he was looking for—the Kentucky Fried Chicken container. And inside it, there it was: the ELF transmitter from Spider Legs that Nancy had stowed there. Harry ripped it out of the box and scrambled from the room.

He rushed back to the truck. As he climbed in, he handed Rachel the ELF.

"What is it?" she said.

"It's an extralow-frequency transmitter," he said. "It's designed to send a signal from Mars, so it should be able to send one from the mine."

Rachel's brows went up in admiration. This man was a step ahead. Then it began to dawn on her why they would need the ELF, and what the need might imply. The mine could mean safety—or a stone-cold tomb.

They drove off.

56

In the foothills down at the base of the mountains, a good ten miles away from the erupting peak, a roadblock had been set up. The Humvees were just now pulling in, bringing the last refugees down from the besieged town.

There was a lot of activity at this crossroads. People being bandaged by paramedics, being eased into ambulances. Neighbors huddling with their arms around each other, commiserating, watching nature's grand, horrifying display, from this safe distance at last. Assorted media people set up and doing excited live broadcasts. More media types arriving on the fly every two minutes, breathless, goggle-eyed.

Nancy, Terry, Stan, and Greg climbed shakily out of the lead Humvee. As their feet touched solid ground—ground that wasn't vibrating constantly—for the first time in twenty-four hours, they looked at each other with relief. Then, as they stood and stretched and gazed up at the mountain and started to talk about Dreyfus and Harry, the mountain upped the ante.

A *big* earthquake hit. Short, limited to eight or nine seconds, but strong—a six point five on the Richter Scale, at least. And then everyone pointed and gasped and shouted. The distant but sharp outlines of Dante's Peak suddenly appeared to blur, to quiver, as though the mountain itself had gone out of focus. Then, the whole southeast slope of the mountain began to slide. And from behind the slide, as it plunged down the mountain at two hundred miles per hour, a gigantic eruption ripped open the volcano to its very guts.

The massive head of superheated steam-charged magma, under tremendous upwelling pressure from below, bursting with incalculable energy and trapped from above, was suddenly released by the landslide. It blew. It expanded logarithmically in nanoseconds. It supernovaed. An explosion flared outward equivalent to the detonation of ten million tons of TNT. One cubic mile of mountain was blown into the air.

And an ungodly roar finally reached the ears of the watchers below. A roar so earthshaking and sustained that tears came to the eyes of those who had lived in the shadow of this no-longer-crouching beast. Tears of sheer, awed, primal fear.

A black ash cloud rose a good twelve miles into the sky.

Bolts of strange-colored lightning streaked the clouds. Blue, green, red.

Even the disaster-hardened police and media types exchanged "God Almighty" glances.

The powerful quake knocked the Forestry Service pickup sideways off the road into a wooden bus shelter that collapsed on impact. Harry downshifted frantically and kept the truck moving forward during the temblor. Once it stopped, he got them back on the road, and was accelerating as much as the naked rims would allow, when the earth gave a vast shudder. It was the southeast slope sliding, an event they couldn't see; it was out of their sight lines.

Then they heard the god-awful roar of the mega-eruption, the top of the mountain blowing off. A roar that literally deafened them—so close were they to the mouth of the beast—for minutes afterward.

Harry floored the accerator, careening the truck out of town and onto the road to the mine. They looked up at the erupting mountain, each of them now almost rigid with fear.

Harry urged more speed out of the truck, willing the vehicle on, visualizing the mine around the next bend, just a quarter mile farther.

He glanced in the mirror and reacted: It couldn't be! He spun around in his seat for a direct look. No! Please!

But it was what he dreaded.

Something awesome was happening in the distance behind and above them. A huge dark cloud stretched from horizon to horizon. The cloud was racing down at them off the mountain. This was a pyroclastic flow—a killer cloud of pumice and white-hot gas and ash moving at six hundred miles an hour.

It was one of the most awe-inspiring sights in all of nature. This much Harry knew: To be in the path of one, to see one racing at you, is to know death before you die. The shock wave of a nuclear bomb is not so utterly deadly.

The pyroclastic cloud billowed like a stupendous hand, clutching at them as it hurtled down, consuming everything in its path.

Going on terrified reflex alone, Harry slewed the truck around the corner at forty miles an hour and, seeing the mine entrance, pointed the truck at it, then locked his hands and prayed.

He tried not to look back. He did—in the passenger side-view mirror. The inky cloud was already right on top of them!! They were toast! They weren't going to make it! Then he saw the printed message: *Objects in mirror are closer than they appear.*

"Hold tight!" Harry yelled, gripping the shuddering wheel with all his strength.

Behind them, the many-times-hurricane-force cloud howled its way into Dante's Peak, an 800-degree-Celsius monster rolling in all its horrible glory, obliterating every material thing. Cluster's motel just vaporized. All the buildings on the main street were suddenly gone. Vehicles stranded on the broken freeway were blasted into oblivion.

The entire town was consumed as by a hydrogen bomb at ground zero.

In split seconds the deadly flow was on the truck, overwhelming it, lifting it up just as it reached the mine. The truck, with all aboard, was literally blasted through the fence, through the sheet-metal doors and into the mine entrance as the cloud rolled up and over the granite hillside and kept going.

Instantly the timbered mine entrance disappeared under blast debris—a rain of rocks, trees, mud, charred timber fragments, and a massive slide of earth from above.

The mine was sealed

57

The truck hit the entrance of the mine with the sound of screaming, tearing metal as the sides were ripped off the vehicle and it finally came to a shattering, grinding halt.

Harry slammed against the windshield, smashing it to pieces. He fell back, bruised and bleeding. But in one piece. As were the others. In shock, they looked around in the sudden relative silence. The roar of the pyroclastic shock wave reverberated, but outside—out there. And they were somehow in here.

The truck completely blocked the mine entrance. Like a cork in a giant bottle.

"Everybody okay?" Harry said, checking his head lacerations, astounded they were still alive.

But they were. Rachel was wiping off Graham's bloody nose. Lauren was rubbing a sore arm, still clutching her crystal. Rachel herself was bruised all over, but had no time now to check herself.

The truck's engine had been knocked dead on impact, but its headlights, miraculously, still worked. They cast a bright, eerie light ahead of them down the length of the mine tunnel.

Outside, cascades of ash and volcanic debris continued to fall over the entrance to the mine, burying everything, including the entrance itself.

The truck occupants tried to gather their wits. Harry stared down the lighted tunnel assessing the possibilities. Even if they'd wanted to, there was no way they could leave the tunnel the way they'd come in.

Harry quickly concluded that their future, if they had one, lay straight ahead. He got his legs up and kicked with his feet, breaking the remaining glass of the shattered windshield.

Once he had made a safe opening, he helped Rachel and the two kids scramble forward onto the hood of the vehicle and out into the tunnel. Roughy followed tentatively onto the hood, then bounded down to the tunnel floor.

At the roadblock down at the foot of the mountains, Nancy, Terry, Greg, and Stan were awed, along with all the other people watching the conflagration from a distance. They had seen the pyroclastic cloud roll down the mountain at frightening speed, and they continued to hear its roar. They knew its power and they knew what it meant: Nobody survives such an onslaught.

Nancy fell to her knees in tears. She buried her face in her hands.

"So long, Harry," Terry said, pounding one of his crutches into the ground.

The defunct silver mine was Graham's private stomping ground, an off-limits clubhouse for him and his running buddies. Now he brought the little band of survivors along the tunnel past several forks and turnings to a small rocky chamber supported by heavy timber uprights and beams. They were old, old creosote-sealed timbers, but they looked sturdy for the most part. Dust filled the air and small landslides of riprap cluttered the corners of the space.

Throughout the chamber was considerable evidence of kids having spent time in secret conclave. Cans of soda, neatly piled; a dartboard nailed to one of the uprights; comic books; a Beck poster; a Game Boy; a half-eaten bag of chips; a nubby-wheeled skateboard; a pair of hightop sneakers. The essentials of a boy's life.

"Here," Graham said, digging in a wooden crate. "Flashlights."

"Graham, is there another way out of here?" Harry said.

Graham shook his head. "I know this mine like the back of my hand," he said. "We're trapped down here."

Graham handed out three flashlights while Lauren, using matches he had given her, lighted some of the plentiful jars of candles.

"There's crackers and chips and some Coke back here," Graham said. He was having very mixed

241

feelings about this wholesale opening of his secret sanctum: proud to be of help in this moment of crisis, irked to be exposed.

Everyone stiffened as they felt renewed volcanic tremors that seemed to go on and on. Then a frightening sound in the distance: parts of the old mine collapsing, echoing along the curving tunnels.

Roughy whimpered and turned around once. She laid her head on her paws and looked scared.

The humans all looked at each other in the flickering candlelight. The mine walls and ceiling were shedding dirt. The ancient cedar pit props were shaking as if they were about to buckle.

"Sounds like this whole place is about to come down on us," Rachel said.

"We're going to be buried alive," Lauren said. She started to cry. Rachel put her arms around her children. There was nothing else she could do.

Then a distant sharp rumble: a part of the tunnel collapsing. One of the props near the entrance to the chamber snapped with a report like gunfire.

Harry remembered the ELF. "I'm going back to the truck for the transmitter," he said. He started away.

"I'll come with you," Graham said. "You might get lost."

"No!" Rachel said. "I'll go. I know the way."

Graham looked at her, stunned. "*You*, Mom?"

"For God sakes, Graham," she said, "you think I listened to my mother when I was a kid?"

Graham looked at his mother in a whole new light. He smiled.

"I'm going alone," Harry said. "You guys stay together."

Rachel smiled apprehensively, her arms still around the kids. Everybody wanted to be brave, but their hearts were sinking.

Lauren said it for all of them. "We're not going to get out, are we?"

Harry forced a big smile. "Sure we are," he said. Then, to bolster the upbeat thought: "Hey, you guys ever been deep-sea fishing?"

They were all surprised by the question.

"No, Harry," Rachel said, forcing a smile.

"I'm not usually real big on taking vacations," he said, "but with you guys along, it'll be great. We'll go down to the Keys, charter a boat, and catch us some big ones. How about it, you up for that?"

Rachel and Harry looked at each other. Like two people who had known each other forever. Rachel smiled. "Sounds like fun, Harry," she said.

Graham tried to get into the spirit of it. "Yeah, Harry," he said, "sounds great."

Little Lauren nodded bravely.

Harry smiled. "Okay then, it's settled," he said. "I'll be back in a flash."

He turned and jogged off down the tunnel, soon disappearing from sight. For a long moment the beam of his flashlight glowed reassuringly way down the tunnel. Then it too disappeared.

All that remained, as Rachel, Graham, Lauren, and Roughy huddled together to wait, and as parts of the mine broke down, were the trembling earth and distant rumblings.

With a sudden terrifying roar of sound, another part of the tunnel very close to them collapsed. A charge of dust came exploding out of the tunnel where Harry had gone. When the dust cleared, there was no light and no sound from that direction.

Up toward the mouth of the mine, the truck head-lights still dimly illuminated a stretch of tunnel.

Harry had rounded a turning and was jogging toward it when he heard a huge, sinister groan right above him and felt dirt fall. The roof of the tunnel was about to give way. Harry was off and running as fast as he could toward the truck. As he ran, the roof of the tunnel behind him collapsed. Then another section, and another, each one threatening to obliterate Harry if he couldn't outrun it.

And he couldn't. The roof came crashing down, and a blizzard of dust, rock, and dirt went flying. Harry put his head down and tried to crash on through it like a tailback. He charged on ahead, five paces, eight, then stumbled and went down under the weight of a falling beam. He disappeared beneath the rubble.

58

Rachel and the kids heard it—the horrible sound they could tell was coming from way out toward the entrance. It surely sounded like the roof caving in on Harry, sealing him off from them.

Fearing the worst, Lauren shouted, "Harry! Harry!"

Fighting tears, Rachel pulled her children to her.

Out front there was only the pile of rubble and silence. The headlights on the Forestry Service pickup gleamed in the distance, growing weaker. A new tremor released a fresh fall of trussed-up earth onto the pile. All was still.

Until . . .

The pile split open and Harry's hand emerged.

Soon he was slowly digging himself out from beneath the rocks and the rubble, grimacing in pain. And when he finally freed himself he looked at his left arm hanging there in an odd way. It was obviously broken.

Harry levered himself to his feet and slogged to the truck. Wincing from the pain and with great, clumsy effort, he squeezed himself through the windshield using only one arm.

He pulled out the flashlight he'd been able to hang on to and shined it around the front seat, the floorboard, looking for the ELF. No sign of it. Then he spied it wedged in the backseat of the truck. Harry was reaching for the ELF when suddenly he heard another disquieting sound. Jesus! What now? he wondered.

But the sound was different this time. A creak? A groan? Something just outside was about to give. Suddenly Harry found out what it was.

BOOM! . . . BOOM!

The doors of the truck suddenly cracked off their frames and began to close in. The very walls of the mine were squeezing in on the truck, gradually squashing it. Harry was caught in the middle as the truck's walls collapsed in closer . . . closer. His broken arm was pinned to his body, and still the walls continued to converge. He was about to be crushed. . . .

And then they stopped. Bits of gravel and dirt fell through the cracked-open roof of the truck, mixing with the sweat on Harry's face. Harry was afraid to move, afraid to breathe.

Then, with great effort and great difficulty, he turned his body around. And spotted it in the beam of his flashlight . . .

The ELF, lodged in the corner, apparently undamaged.

He struggled to reach for it, coming close to passing out from the pain. He stretched and wriggled and inched his lanky body forward in the impossibly narrow space. A metal casket, he thought as dizziness took over. This is where I'll die. Within inches of . . .

And everything went black—

He came to. He was still there, stretched out, wedged in a vise. He gathered all his strength and made a huge lunge and got his fingertips on the ELF. He scratched and scrabbled it toward him . . . He had it in his grasp! He pulled it to him hungrily. Searched for the switch. Flipped it.

Nothing happened.

He flipped it again.

Again!

He flooded with anger. It didn't work! The damn multimillion-dollar piece of NASA hardware didn't work! He'd been pouring tax dollars into the hands of imbecile government incompetents! And with that he banged the ELF against the wall of the truck with all his diminished strength.

And the red light turned on.

The ELF was transmitting. Harry's face brightened, then lighted up at least his section of the tunnel.

59

It was gray, early dawn, with a light ashfall still in the air. But the whole area around the mine entrance was illuminated by so many klieg lights, it was like high noon.

A big, olive drab National Guard chopper settled into the scene, joining a swarm of rescue equipment: bulldozers, backhoes, tunnel borers, earth movers. There were National Guardsmen, rescue workers and so many press people one might have thought it was a movie premiere or an Elvis sighting.

All eyes were on the entrance to the mine as the workers gingerly shored up the final section and cleared out the remaining yards of rubble.

An access tunnel was open. The way was clear. A mine worker came out first . . . Then came Rachel, the kids, and finally Roughy.

The workers, the media and other onlookers burst into spontaneous applause as the rescue workers escorted them out of the mine.

They were caked with mud and grime, and half-blinded by the glare of the lights, but otherwise they were okay.

Paramedics wrapped them in blankets as reporters swarmed around, calling out questions. The Guardsmen tried to keep them at bay.

Harry, leaning against the ambulance with his broken arm in a sling, was having his cuts and lacerations worked on by a paramedic when he saw them emerge. He pushed past the paramedic and made a beeline.

"I'm not finished!" the paramedic said.

But Harry was not listening. He was pushing his way through the crowd.

Rachel saw Harry first. Her face lit up with surprise. And with pure, unadulterated joy.

Then Lauren saw him, and Graham.

"Look, it's Harry!" he said. "He's alive!"

He and Rachel were standing before each other, two people who'd gone through hell together.

Then Rachel was in his arms. They held on to each other with all their might. The children joined them, and Harry wrapped his arms around them, too. There were no words.

Until Graham found a few. "We thought you were dead," he said.

A National Guard Humvee made its way into the cordoned-off area and came to a stop. Its doors opened and Terry, Nancy, Greg, and Stan jumped out shouting

Harry's name, then came rushing over. They patted Harry's back and hugged him and pumped his hand.

"Harry, when I saw that ELF light blinking," Terry said, "I almost fell out of my chair."

"He started screaming, 'Thank you, NASA! Thank you!' " Nancy said.

Harry looked around. "Where's Paul?" he said.

A moment's silence. "Paul didn't make it," Terry said.

"No!" Harry said, reacting as though somebody had punched him hard.

They all looked at each other grimly.

Finally Terry said, "Hell, at least he got to see the show."

"The show," Harry said quietly. "The damned show."

And with that, Harry put his arms around Rachel and the kids.

The rescue workers protected them from the reporters as the guardsmen escorted them to the waiting HUEY. They clambered aboard. The pilot jacked up the power, the blades turned, picked up speed; and the bird shot into the air.

Harry, Rachel, the kids, and an excited Roughy were lifted away from the spot that had come so close to being their tomb but had in fact been their salvation.

Soon the copter was banking over Dante's Peak. As they swept above the town, so recently an ideal place to live good lives, they saw the full extent of the awesome devastation the volcano had wrought.

To Harry, it seemed to be screaming a stark message: The grand and formative processes of nature marched according to dictates larger than man's, and laughed at such humble ideas as "home."

He stared at the devastation morosely. Then . . .

Nature be damned, he thought. Nature in this powerful, heedless form is my enemy! And I'll continue to battle her and poke her and pick her apart until I can get the jump on her. Until no more people die by ambush and blind mayhem.

He took Rachel's hand and they both looked down, grateful to be alive. Grateful for each other.

The chopper banked and climbed steeply away from the scene of horror, and raised them up high enough for the majestic, green-forested Cascades to take on their benign appearance once again.